Princess By Mistake

Aurelia Skye

Published by Amourisa Press, 2016.

PRINCESS BY MISTAKE

First edition. January 12, 2016.

Copyright © 2016 Aurelia Skye.

ISBN: 979-8223935155

Written by Aurelia Skye.

What started out as the worst day ever just got worse. Incorrectly identified as her strange roommate, curvy Jory finds herself spirited away by an intergalactic bounty hunter intent on returning her to the prince she's expected to marry. Except she's no princess, and forget a prince when she could have the sexy, magenta-skinned alien instead—if he'll accept she's a mistaken princess and give in to the desire simmering between them.

Chapter One

DESPITE THE EARLY HOUR, not quite even eleven a.m., Jory Wilson was ready to declare this day officially the worst one ever. It had started with an early meeting, necessitating leaving her comfy home office to commute into the city. Instead of her usual fleece sweatpants, she had donned pantyhose that required way too much effort, along with a neat pinstripe pencil skirt that always made her rounded butt look a little too bubbly for her tastes. *En route* to the meeting, she had stepped down from a curb and broken the heel off one of her new shoes, while also twisting her ankle, though not to the point where she couldn't walk on it.

She had taken the train, fighting her way through the crowd to find a spot, not lucky enough to secure a seat. She had clung to the strap as usual and endured the close crush of people around her. As she'd neared her stop for the office, some bozo had squeezed her butt, pinching hard enough for her to squeal.

In a huff, she had stormed off the subway, glaring at the other passengers as she tried to identify the ass-grabber. The mystery remained unsolved, and she had rushed up the stairs of the platform to street-level, crossing the last two blocks on her broken heel with an awkward gait.

Upon arriving at the office, Jory had discovered she was called to the meeting under false pretenses. Ostensibly, it had been to discuss her future with the company, and she had expected the raise and promotion she'd been promised more than a year ago. Instead, she had learned her job was being outsourced to India, and she was expected to train her replacement via telecommuting at a reduced rate of pay.

Jory had stared at them in surprise and more than a little anger. They didn't seem to understand why she was upset about training her replacement and losing her promised promotion. Unable to control her temper, which was often a failing of hers, she had let loose on her boss, his boss, and their boss. It had been an ugly meeting and left her no doubt she wouldn't receive a good reference from the company when she began job hunting again.

Fortunately, Jory had a side gig editing and writing for an independent magazine, and she had been saving her money for a while, so there was no rush to find a new job as a corporate drone. That was little consolation for having lost the promotion for which she had slaved for the past year.

By the time she arrived home—hot, frazzled, and in no mood for more irritations—finding the door partially open was the last straw. It wasn't the first time her strange roommate, Chiara, had left the door unlocked, but it was the first time she had left the apartment in such disarray. It looked like a tornado had blown through, and Jory stared in shock. Housekeeping was not her favorite thing, and the idea of having to pick up all the mess irritated her.

She strode through the clutter, too focused on delivering a piece of her mind directly to Chiara to worry about taking off her broken shoe. She wished she had the luxury of evicting the other woman. With the recent status change to unemployed, and the fact Chiara always paid her rent on time—strangely enough, the first time she had tried to pay rent with a handful of diamonds—Jory knew she was still stuck with the other woman. That didn't mean she couldn't lay down a few laws and make it plain what was and was not acceptable behavior.

For example, inviting strangers to sleep on the sofa was unacceptable. Jory stared at the large form currently sprawled across her small sofa. He was a behemoth of muscles even in a supine position. Long blond hair trailed across his shoulder and down his chest, and she found herself drawing nearer him to examine his features more closely.

He had a strong brow, straight nose, and lips that were just a shade too full. The kind of lips that invited kissing.

Jory blinked at that random thought, abstractly amused that she found herself contemplating making out with the stranger who was asleep on her couch. More than likely, the man was just as strange as Chiara, and even more likely, he was with her roommate in a romantic sense. Not that the other woman had ever brought back boyfriends or dates to the apartment, but then again, Jory didn't often do so either. Men tended to avoid her curvy frame, quick temper, and smart mouth. It was a dynamite combination prone to sudden explosion, as her mother liked to say in a teasing fashion.

As Jory bent over the form of the sleeping man, preparing to shake his shoulder to wake him, his eyes snapped open. She drew in a halting breath at the beautiful purple irises, rimmed by darker purple rings. She'd never seen anything so stunning or strange in all her life. They had to be colored contacts, right?

Blinking aside her temporary mesmerism, she forced herself to sound brusque when she asked, "Who are you, and what are you doing in my apartment?"

The stranger sat up abruptly, forcing Jory to scramble backward and almost land on her butt. She caught herself at the last moment, teetering on the uneven heels, and glared up at him. Way, way up. The man towered over her by at least a foot-and-a-half, and she wasn't exactly short at five-six. Jory stretched her neck backward in an effort to meet his gaze, and her eyes widened at the sight of a device flipping up above his eye. "What is that?" There had been nothing on his face a second ago.

He didn't bother to answer, but a shutter on the apparatus spun open, revealing a small red dot that grew to a beam barely thicker than a pencil. Jory gasped with outrage as the light scanned her from head to toe. It didn't hurt, but it was a violation of some sort, and just plain freaky—like Chiara and all the other oddities that had come with having the woman as her roommate for the last seven months. Job or no job, money or no money, Chiara was going to have to leave if she persisted in bringing home weirdoes like this guy.

Jory racked her brain, trying to remember if there was some kind of convention in the city that would draw the cosplayers and tech types like this guy. He had to be wearing some kind of strange costume, and she was more convinced than ever when the light around him sort of flickered, and a flash of magenta seemed to superimpose itself over his skin, giving him a red-pink tinge, before another flicker restored his normal appearance.

She shook her head. "What is going on here? Where's Chiara?"

The man stared at her for a long moment, still silent, and leaving her wondering if he could actually speak at all. She supposed with lips and eyes like that, he didn't have to talk much to get the ladies' attention, but she was more concerned about his intentions than how attractive he was at the moment. "Answer me. You know what, it doesn't matter who you are, or what you're doing here. Just get the heck out of my apartment before I call the police."

The man lifted his hand, as though about to check his watch. At the last moment, Jory realized it was like no timepiece she had ever seen before. The cuff looked like a combination of plastic, metal, and some shiny skin—perhaps lizard, though she couldn't think of any lizard that was naturally a blue-violet shade.

Another one of those strange apparatuses popped out of it, but this time it didn't emit a red light. Instead, a sickly yellow cloud of gas erupted from his wristband, surrounding her in a millisecond. Before she even had the thought of holding her breath or trying to escape the miasma, it had entered into her lungs, nose, and mouth.

A giddy, lightheaded sensation, similar to the first wave of euphoria from nitrous oxide at the dentist, swept over Jory. She started to fall and let out a little cry of alarm.

Teetering on the broken heel, she grasped desperately for something to break her fall. To her surprise, it was the solidly muscled arms of the stranger who had just gassed her that enfolded her, keeping her from hitting the floor. Even as unconsciousness swept over her, she couldn't help noticing how well-built the stranger was. It was a strange thought, to be admiring or appreciating anything about her attacker.

ZANDAR HEFTED THE PRINCESS over his shoulder with no effort at all. She looked different from the photo he'd been given, but he liked this softer, rounder version of Chiondri. Most women on Gentarres and Karadis were built like athletes or warriors—either lean or muscled, but almost exclusively tall. He could see why the prince so admired this woman from the Royal House of Cardiff. If he had the opportunity to bed such a female, he wouldn't hesitate.

Already exhausted from the urgent speed at which he had moved upon receiving this assignment, his thoughts were on the muddled side. Even the small nap he'd risked taking at the princess's Earth dwelling hadn't restored him completely. He had to nip such thoughts about the royal over his shoulder in the bud before his diminished state led him to do something disallowed by his contract. His mission was to return the princess to her affianced and collect his bounty, not seduce the next queen of his father's home planet.

Even knowing he shouldn't admire the princess couldn't keep his pants from growing uncomfortably tight as he switched her to a more comfortable position so he could reach the transporter button on his wrist cuff. Still holding her, he stepped out onto the balcony and into his waiting pod. Cloaked by advanced technology, the vessel was invisible to NASA or other agencies that might be able to detect spacecraft orbiting Earth.

The tiny pod was just big enough for the two of them, and she had to sit on his lap. It was a damned shame, he thought with a grin, as her curves melted against him. Like the pod, the larger vessel had the same cloaking technology, and they docked with it and stepped aboard without any of Earth's officials being any the wiser to the shuttle's presence.

In his opinion, it was a heap of junk, but he'd been forced to accept it as part of the assignment to retrieve the princess. What the harbinger-class ship lacked in defense, it made up for in speed. He couldn't deny it was faster than his own ship, but he was still not happy about having to use the royal vessel.

Once on the bridge of the small ship, designed to be manned by one person, he shifted his hold on Chiondri once more and strode down the hallway to the small room that passed for a medical bay. He didn't expect there to be any long-term side effects from gassing her, but it was as good a place as any to dump her—and hopefully out of sight and out of mind.

He couldn't allow himself to dwell on the tempting curves of the princess, or the sweetly rounded face whose skin was so soft when he gave in to the impulse to stroke a finger down her cheek. Framed by a long fall of chestnut-brown hair, it was a classically beautiful face.

Her lips were full and soft when he ran his thumb across them, and he contemplated bending to taste her. His pants grew tighter still, but he forced himself to resist the urge, not just because she was the future bride of the Royal Prince of Gentarres, but also because it was more than a little disturbing to admire her this way while she was out cold.

With a decisive nod, he turned away from the table where she lay to return to the bridge, trying to block out the memory of her vivid green eyes as he sat down behind the navigation console. It didn't take long to disengage the autopilot and set them on a course for Gentarres. He would have the princess returned to her eager groom within days, thanks to the speed of the harbinger-class.

That meant three days of being around the temptation of the sweet princess, who seemed anything but sweet from the few moments already spent in her company when she was conscious. His mouth quirked as he recalled her outrage and her continuous questions he hadn't bothered to answer.

It shouldn't be a shock to her that her fiancé had sent a bounty hunter to collect the woman. Their marriage had been arranged since before either was born, and there wasn't one thing either Chiondri or Kendrick could do to escape their union. Zandar still didn't know why the princess had pulled a runner just days before the royal wedding, and he knew Kendrick was just as baffled as he was about the turn of events.

He briefly wondered why Kendrick hadn't moved up the wedding just so he could indulge in the taste of his new bride. Her sweetly rounded ass would be a perfect fit for the size of his palms, and he could easily imagine holding her against the wall and sinking his cock into her slick heat.

Suppressing a groan, he reminded himself why that couldn't happen and returned his attention to more mundane matters, like piloting the ship that barely needed any sentient assistance once the route was programmed. He waited for the princess to awaken, dreading the next confrontation with her, fully expecting her to demand he return her to Earth or some other backward planet so she could hide from the royal family of Gentarres.

She would probably plead, cajole, threaten, and offer money. She might even put forward her sweet curves to manipulate him into doing her bidding. His brow beaded with sweat at the thought, and he firmly told himself she didn't have a chance in hell of convincing him to abandon his duty, no matter the incentive. He would just have to make that clear to her—and himself.

Chapter Two

JORY SLEPT BETTER THAN she had for a long time. The fact was she couldn't remember ever feeling so rested when she stretched and yawned before opening her eyes. It took a moment to realize she wasn't staring at the plain white walls of her apartment, and there was no sun streaming through the window as there should be.

When she turned her head to the left, she could see vast darkness all around her, highlighted by streaks of blue-white. It reminded her of the documentary she had seen of electric jellyfish floating in the darkness of the ocean, their tendrils trailing behind them as they floated along. Something shimmering obstructed her view, and it was like peering through a lenticular puzzle. As it dawned on her she was looking out into space through some strange material that kept her separated from the vacuum, she shook her head.

Panic overwhelmed her, making it difficult to breathe, she panted as she tried to draw in a deep breath. Finally, when her chest felt like it would explode, she was able to inhale and then exhale raggedly. Once lung function had been restored, a piercing shriek escaped her as she mentally rejected what she was seeing. In seconds, the strange man burst into the room, his hand at his side, resting on a holster that presumably held some sort of weapon.

She couldn't believe what was happening to her, and the most likely explanation was the gas he had used. "What did you do to me?" Her head spun as she sat up on the metal table, gesturing toward the wall-like membrane separating them from the *illusion* of space. It had to be illusion, after all, because nothing else made sense. It was simply some strange hallucinogenic hangover effect from whatever gas he had poisoned her with earlier that day. Was she dying? "What did you do to me?" she demanded again.

"Calm down, princess. You can save the hysterics for Prince Kendrick. I'm not being paid enough to deal with them." His hand fell away from the gun at his side, as he stared at her when he crossed his arms over his massive chest.

Jory stared at him in confusion, deciding she had to relegate the space hallucination to the back of her mind and focus on whatever was unfolding before her. She could indulge in panic later. "I just don't understand what's going on here. Who are you? What do you want with me? Why have you kidnapped me?"

The tall large stranger shook his head, his too-full lips quirking with a hint of amusement.

It was then that Jory realized the hallucinogenic effect had spread beyond the imaginary walls of this make-believe spaceship to the man himself. Where before he'd had golden-brown skin and blond hair, his skin was now a shade of magenta, and his long hair was more silver than blond. Instead of making him look old, the gorgeous color had the contradictory effect of being vibrant and sexy. His purple eyes were still the same as they had been back at her apartment, ringed with deep purple that made her heart rate accelerate even under the circumstances.

As he turned slightly to the side, she gasped at the sight of a tail extending from the back of his pants. It snaked around his thigh and rested with just the tip vibrating, almost the same way as her cat's when he was really excited. Or about to pounce.

Feeling woozy, Jory slumped against the table again. "What is going on?" She stared up at him, surprised to see a trace of sympathy in his expression. "What did you give me, you hulking behemoth? Why am I seeing things? Will this effect wear off?"

He frowned, looking confused. "Seeing things? What kind of things?"

She laughed, and it held a sharp edge of hysteria. "You wouldn't believe me if I told you."

He arched a silvery blond brow. "Try me, princess."

With that same hysterical laugh, Jory pointed to the wall, or what passed for a wall in her hallucinogenic state. "For one thing, it looks like we're in the middle of space in a see-through ship." She waved at him, pointing to his thigh area. "And for another, you've turned reddish-pink and sprouted a tail. See how crazy that is?"

His frown deepened. "I should run a diagnostic on you, princess. You shouldn't have these kinds of side effects from the gas, but you're clearly confused. Or a good actor," he muttered under his breath, but just loud enough for her to hear.

She glared at him, irritated he could think she was making this up when he was the one who had kidnapped her. Somehow, Jory made herself sit still while the apparatus above his eye flicked into view, having been invisible just seconds before. That same light scanned over her again. After a moment, he nodded, looking satisfied. "Well?" she asked when he didn't speak.

He shrugged his large shoulders. "You're in perfect health, Chiondri. I don't know why you feel confused or dazed. Perhaps it's the adjustment of space travel after being on Earth. The radiation levels on that planet, coupled with the oxygen content, air pollution, and chemical residue, are enough to alter anyone's brain functions. I know it played hell with my holo-suit, and I'm sure my human holographic projection flickered a couple of times around Earthlings."

His lips curved into a mischievous smile. "I ran across the path of a woman in leather and piercings, who took one look at me and screamed, so I assume she must have seen my true form."

Her head pounded ferociously at his words as she tried to make sense of them. "Wait, are you trying to claim you're some kind of space man?"

Slowly, the man stood up straighter and took a step toward her. "I don't know what game you're playing, princess, but there's no need and no point. I won't be manipulated, and I have a mission to complete. Once I dump you back on Kendrick's lap, you'll be his problem and not mine. In the meantime, save the head games."

"Why the hell do you keep calling me princess? I'm not a princess. I'm about as far from a princess as you can get. I'm probably more like a serf." The man was clearly out of his mind. Not that she had doubted that anyway, because sane people didn't go around kidnapping other people and gassing them and...well, doing whatever was he was with this production.

He laughed. "Nice try, princess, but you can drop the act. I don't know why you didn't want to marry Kendrick, and it's not my concern. All I have to do is get you back to the palace, and you can work it out with him — though I wouldn't expect any kind of resolution besides ending up as the Royal bride if I were you. You know how these treaties and marriage contracts work between royal houses and warring planets."

Jory drew her brows together. "I'm not playing any game with you. I don't know what's going on here, or what kind of setup you're preparing for, but I want it to end right now. If you want ransom of some sort, you've taken the wrong girl, because I come from what you would call humble roots. My mom is a baker, and my dad is dead. There aren't any rich grandparents or anyone else to scrape together millions of dollars to rescue me from your insanity."

A ferocious scowl compressed his features. "I don't know what you hope to gain by this, but I'm done with your shenanigans, princess. You can sit here in the medical bay playing head games with yourself, or you can move about the ship, but stay out of my way."

With that pronouncement, he turned on his heel and strode from the room where he had left her. It was getting harder to pretend hallucinogenic side effects of the gas were responsible for what she observed around her. If this was all a set-up, he had gone all-out to make it seem authentic. Her head whirled with confusion as she tried to comprehend that this could really be happening to her.

As she leaned against the metal table, she realized it certainly explained a lot about her strange roommate, Chiara. The woman had always been odd and seemed completely clueless about social niceties, manners, and customs. Jory had always chalked it up to a strange upbringing or something, because she didn't have any further information. Her roommate wasn't exactly the sharing type, so they had remained as roommates rather than friends.

Jory remembered the first week they had lived together when she had walked in to the kitchen to find her roommate scrubbing ice off the side of the freezer and practically inhaling it by the handful. It was strange, but she'd tried to be polite and ignore it. Her roommate definitely had strange dietary habits, like always eating the bones along with the chicken.

Could it be Chiara was really some kind of alien princess hiding out on Earth to avoid an arranged marriage? Even as she had the idea, Jory thought she had gone completely round the bend, though she could find no other explanation for how she'd ended up in this situation.

Supposing she accepted the theory her roommate was an alien, it still didn't explain why the strange man, whose name she really needed to learn, had kidnapped her instead of Chiara. If ever there was a case of mistaken identity, this had to be it.

She just had to convince him of that, so he could return her to her home planet, where she could undergo years of therapy to try to convince herself none of this had ever happened. With the goal firmly in mind, Jory left the medical bay and walked down the corridor.

The decor was at least a familiar sight, with industrial-looking utilitarian metal beams and white tile. Jory cautiously made her way forward, pausing at each of the few doors to peer inside. Most revealed nothing of interest, and a couple didn't open at all. They bore pads beside the hydraulic doors that appeared to be biometric scanners. When she pressed her hand against the first one she encountered, nothing happened.

With a shrug, Jory continued down the hallway until it opened into a large room, which she entered hesitantly. The large man sat behind what looked like a complicated console with buttons and flashing lights straight from a science fiction movie. Hesitantly, she cleared her throat. His shoulders stiffened, but he didn't look in her direction. "Excuse me, sir, but could you please talk to me?"

Slowly, he spun his chair toward her. Even sitting down and across the room, he was still intimidating. She forced herself to walk nearer to him, swallowing down the nervous twist of nausea rising up her esophagus. When she was close, but not quite within touching range, she said, "First, what's your name?"

"Zandar."

She nodded to show her acknowledgment before plunging into her explanation. "I think there's been a misunderstanding, Mr. Zandar."

"Just Zandar," he said abruptly.

She nodded again. "Well, all right then, Zandar—I think there has been some kind of mix-up. It seems to me it's a case of mistaken identity. I mean, assuming my roommate is actually some kind of alien princess on the run from her arranged bridegroom—which is a pretty big leap of faith, but who am I to argue in this situation?" She cleared her throat and attempted to marshal her thoughts again, almost losing place in the face of his skepticism. "Seriously, Zandar, I'm not Princess Chiara or whoever you're looking for. I am just plain Jory Wilson, and it appears I've been caught up in some kind of intergalactic case of faulty identification."

His lips quirked. "That is certainly an interesting theory, princess, except your DNA matches the DNA profile stored in my scanner."

She shook her head, unwilling to believe that. "There has to be some kind of mistake. Your computer must have misread it, or maybe they gave you the wrong DNA sample?"

"A sample that just happens to match some random Earth woman's?" He outright laughed at the idea, his mockery stinging her pride.

Her temper was rising faster than the surge of nausea, and she stomped her foot, unable to resist the childish urge. "Look, I don't have a logical explanation for any of this, but I'm not some princess from another planet. I know where I was born, who my parents are, where I live, and every guy I've ever fucked—which certainly doesn't include an alien prince. I've never been engaged and definitely not to the Royal Prince of the House of Gin Drinkers."

"Gentarres," corrected Zandar, his lips twitching. He was still clearly amused, but reined in the mockery. "I suppose the explanation is plausible, but it's difficult to do."

"What's difficult?"

"Fooling the scanner to read your DNA as someone else's. It would mean the original person had to implant a biochip somewhere on you, and that biochip has to respond to the right frequency to subvert the data stored in the computer, which is pretty tightly secured, and rewrite the programming to match the DNA profile for which I was searching."

Jory frowned, finding the whole idea ridiculously complicated. In light of everything else that had happened to her today, it still didn't seem completely impossible. How crazy was *that*? "If your people can master space travel, surely you can master fooling a computer to recognize my DNA profile as Chiara's?"

He tilted his head, appearing to be deep in thought. Finally, he nodded forcefully. "Very well, princess. I'm willing to indulge you, so let's scan to see if you have a biochip implanted somewhere in your body."

A surge of hope filled Jory at his acquiescence, and she nodded eagerly. "It's the only thing that makes sense."

His lips quirked before his expression went blank. "In that case, strip."

ZANDAR WATCHED WITH barely contained mirth at the rush of emotions that crossed the princess's face. Any second now, he expected her to abandon this ploy and perhaps pursue a different tactic. She had latched onto the biochip explanation all too easily, and while it was possible, it was extremely difficult for anyone to perform the task unless they had intimate knowledge of the programming language used to create the computer database utilized by Gentarres and many other intergalactic systems. To his knowledge, Princess Chiondri had no such background in artificial intelligence or programming.

He had tossed out the idea of her stripping off her clothes as a way to shock her and halt her attempts to manipulate him, but he was the one who ended up shocked. Zandar watched as she bit her lip, and he almost groaned at the thought of taking that soft flesh between his own teeth, biting down with just enough force to make her yelp before soothing the slightly sore spot with the tip of his tongue.

His eyes widened with shock when her hands went to the jacket she wore, and she slid it off her shoulders with obvious reluctance. A silk cami underneath revealed more of her bounteous assets than it hid, and his cock hardened as she reached behind her, apparently intent on unzipping the skirt. The motion thrust her breasts forward and emphasized their generous size. His hands twitched to reach out and grasp them. He'd love to cradle those swollen globes in his palms.

He watched silently as she unfastened the zipper on her skirt, and the striped material slid down her curvy legs, pooling in a heap of fabric at her ankles. She kicked off the broken heel and the other shoe before stepping out of the whole skirt and standing before him in just the cami, pantyhose, and a pair of bright pink panties. His mouth watered at the hint of her shadowy cleft through the lace and silk.

She stood awkwardly, her arms crossed over her breasts in a way he suspected she thought hid them, but only pushed up the cleavage to be more visible. "Is that enough? Can you do the scan?"

For just a second, he contemplated telling her to take off the rest of her clothes, but he knew that would be a bad idea. She was already more than he could resist in her current state of undress, and the thought of having all that creamy flesh opened to his view and his touch made his cock ache and his conscience twinge. He had no claim to this woman and no right to look at her or caress her. That didn't mean his dick accepted any of that knowledge.

Zandar nodded his head. "That'll do. Just hold still." With what he hoped was a brusque and businesslike manner, he activated his scanner system, and the device flipped up above his eye. A second later, the red light engulfed Jory, scanning her from head to toe. The scan yielded the same results as earlier, but there was such a look of determination on her face that he found himself questioning his own confidence for the first time.

Was it possible she had been mistaken for the princess, that somehow Chiondri had planned for this eventuality and chosen her roommate as a dupe? With a frown, Zandar switched to a different mode for a deeper diagnostic. Again, the computer yielded the result she was Chiondri, but with less certainty. It was no longer one hundred percent. Ninety-eight percent was still within standard parameters, but just enough to make him question if the woman before him was really the princess.

She arched a brow. "Can I put my clothes on now, Zandar?"

He nodded abruptly, barely resisting the urge to watch her bend over as she reached for the skirt, knowing he couldn't withstand temptation if he saw more of her breasts. As it was, he wanted to pin her to the wall and take her with rough intensity, until they were both screaming with release. The possibility that she might not be the princess made his desire all the more extreme, because there would be no restrictions on her and no barriers preventing him from taking this Earth woman as his lover.

He glanced at her again when she cleared her throat, finding her dressed in everything except for the broken shoe and its intact mate. "The scan is inconclusive, princess. The results are nominal, but not as definitive as I would prefer. I'm willing to entertain the idea you might be someone other than Princess Chiondri."

"I'm not Princess Chiondri. I don't even know who that is. My roommate's name is Chiara, and she is one strange person. The more I think about it, the more it makes sense that she's an alien."

He sighed, running a hand through his hair. "The thing is, princess, I don't have sophisticated enough equipment to do a proper scan for a biochip, so you're going to have to come with me to Gentarres and sort it out with them there."

She scowled. "Can't you just take me back to Earth and pick up Chiara instead?"

He shook his head. "No, I can't do that. My job is to bring you in, and until I know for sure you aren't Princess Chiondri, I have to act on the assumption you are."

"But if I'm not Chiondri—and I'm not—think of all the extra time you'll have wasted by taking me to that planet when I'm not the one you really want."

He could've disabused her of that notion right away. She was most certainly the one he wanted, the one his cock called for and his body craved. Zandar was almost embarrassed by how much he hoped she really wasn't the princess, but he had been honest with her about protocol.

He had to take her to Gentarres to unravel the mystery of her imprecise DNA identification and establish her identity. She had a valid point that he would be delayed if she wasn't the princess, but his orders were clear, and he knew Kendrick would not be angry with him for proceeding as though this was the princess.

All he had to go on was the single photo he'd been given and Kendrick's description of the princess, which had included scant details such as brown hair and green eyes. The woman in front of him was clearly a match by that vague description, but he imagined there were a million other Earth women who would fit it as well.

If Chiondri had been thinking ahead, and she had planned all along to find someone to be her dupe, perhaps she had even gone looking for a woman who closely resembled her. He had dismissed her as a vapid, airheaded aristocrat, as was typical with most of the royal families of the galaxy, but perhaps there was more substance to Chiondri than he had realized.

And if this woman in front of him really was Chiondri, she certainly had a flair for the dramatic and an unrivaled acting ability, because he was starting to believe she really wasn't the princess. *Or hoping*, whispered a small voice in the back of his mind, accompanied by several visuals of what he would like to do to the woman before him. "What is your name, if it isn't Chiondri?" For the time being, he would indulge her, hoping for the best outcome — that she wasn't really the princess and could be claimed as his lover.

"I'm Jory Wilson, as I said before. I mistakenly thought you were paying attention." She gave him a saccharine smile.

He laughed at the small dig. "Pardon my attention for wandering in the face of your...assets. You certainly are a dynamite combination, princess."

Her eyes widened, and she blinked at him, looking a little frightened. "Why would you say that?"

With a shrug, he frowned at her. "It was just an observation, princess."

She exhaled raggedly, and her shoulders slowly relaxed. "Okay, it's just my mom says that sometimes too, when she wants to tease me. This whole experience has made me paranoid, I guess. I was starting to think you'd been following me around for months or years and watching my every move."

"Don't worry, *Jory*," He said her name with special emphasis, "It would be my pleasure to watch your every move, but I'm innocent of that accusation." He allowed a little bit of the desire he felt for her to show in his expression, and when she gasped lightly, he knew she had correctly interpreted what he wasn't saying. With a wink in her direction, he turned back to the nav console, tossing ?? over his shoulder, "Make yourself comfortable, Princess Jory, and we will soon be on Gentarres, where you can try to sell your mistaken identity theory to Prince Kendrick."

JORY STARED AT THE alien in shock, certain she must have misunderstood him. It had to be a disconnect or a failed translation from his native alien language. He couldn't really desire her, could he? On Earth, he would have been a professional athlete or an actor, perhaps even one of those muscled wrestlers—which was also a type of actor—and certainly never would have looked twice at a curvy woman like herself. She blinked, at a loss how to respond. Finally, she asked, "How long until we get to Gem Taros?"

"Gentarres," he said, speaking slowly, as if to emphasize each syllable for her slow brain. "The journey should take three days."

"What am I supposed to do with myself for three days on this ship, Zandar?"

He twitched his brow in a suggestive manner, and his lips quirked with barely suppressed amusement. "I'm sure you can think of something, Princess Jory."

"Why do you keep calling me princess? I told you I'm not her." God, this man was frustrating. Apparently, that was a universal truth across all alien species, be they Earth men or Generous Tears...or whatever.

Zandar smiled—the kind of slow, sensuous smile that instantly dampened her panties. "I have a difficult time believing you aren't a princess, Jory. If you aren't the princess I was hired to find, you must still surely be a princess on your world?"

She didn't know whether to giggle like a schoolgirl or bray like a donkey at the extravagant compliment. "I'm definitely not princess material. If you knew anything about Earth, you'd know that. I'm not exactly what you'd call an ideal beauty back home."

"Your planet has strange standards of beauty then, Princess Jory."

Flushed with embarrassment, she struggled to find something else to stare at without looking like she was deliberately avoiding his gaze, though she was. She couldn't believe how flustered the compliments made her and suspected it was the source.

Of course other men had complimented her, and she'd believed some were sincere, but none of those guys had been as overwhelmingly attractive as the huge alien before her. Finally, she summoned the nerve to look at him again, tilting her head to the side. "Are you from Jen Taros too, Zandar?"

"Gentarres," he said again, with a faint hint of impatience. After hesitating for a second, he nodded. "Yes, I'm a Gentarren, but I'm also Karadisian, which is my mother's people, and Karadis is where I feel most at home."

"And what are the Karadisians?" She made sure to pronounce that one correctly, since it seemed important to him. "How did your parents meet if they're from different planets?" Was interplanetary travel no harder than going from Los Angeles to New York City by their standards?

He shrugged a shoulder. "We're from a nearby sector, and my mother was on a galactic tour after finishing her education. She met my father on Gentarres, indulged in a whirlwind affair, and returned home to Karadis when it was over, expecting me."

"Do you spend much time with your dad?"

His expression closed. "Not especially, and that's fine by me. He doesn't approve of my nomadic lifestyle, or my embracing the bounty hunter lifestyle preferred by many of my Karadisian relatives. He feels it's beneath his family name, so I don't bother to use it."

She nodded, sympathy stirring that she quickly suppressed in light of his cool tone and aloof expression. "So, you, uh...have surnames in your planet? Surname is like a last name or second name." What a stupid question, but her brain refused to properly function in such close proximity to Zandar.

His lips twitched. "I'm aware of what a surname is, Princess Jory. To answer your question, the Gentarrens have about fourteen familial names they tack on to first names, and the Karadis people typically use about three."

"What's your full name then?"

"Zandar Gadrick Tel'Afric." The syllables rolled off his tongue in a melodic sound, with an elegant pronunciation she didn't think she could emulate.

With an appreciative glance down his body, she said "Only three names? A big guy like you could probably handle fourteen or fifteen."

He chuckled, and there was definitely a sexual aspect to the sound. "I find handling more than three is a challenge best reserved for the younger crowd."

She blinked. "Is three the typical number on your planet?"

He chuckled. "There is no typical, Jory." It was obvious neither of them was talking about the number of names any longer. "Some require fifty or more, while others are content with a smaller number."

"What about you?" she asked in a breathy whisper, disquieted by how much she wanted to hear his answer, but only if it wasn't something outlandish like fifty.

"One," he said softly. "When you know what you're doing, and you have the one you want, that's more than enough."

Jory barely held in a girlish giggle, kind of in shock that she was flirting with the alien who had kidnapped her and still didn't quite believe she wasn't the princess he sought. The atmosphere was getting thick, and her panties were a sodden mess, necessitating a quick change of subject. "Why doesn't Chiara want to marry this prince Kendrick?"

He shrugged. "I don't know. Everything appeared to be in place for the ceremony, and then she just disappeared a few days before they were set to join. At first, Kendrick believed she had been kidnapped, but when she started running from the people he sent to find her, it was obvious she was deliberately fleeing."

"Is Kendrick cruel? Did he treat her badly or plan to keep forty-nine mistresses after the marriage?" A dart of sympathy spread through her as she imagined Chiara in a situation like that, and she couldn't blame the other woman for having tried to escape. She shuddered. "I can't imagine being forced to marry someone I don't know or don't love just because someone else said I had to."

"That's the way of royalty." Zandar shrugged. "I don't suppose she'll find a way out of it in the end." He arched a brow. "Unless she can convince the tracker she isn't really Princess Chiondri." He winked at her.

Jory managed a small laugh. "Maybe she'll be as lucky as me. You know, without the whole four days there and back just to verify what I've told you a million times — I'm not a princess."

Zandar took a step closer to her, his hand hovering near her cheek for a second before he used two fingers to brush back tendrils of chestnut hair trailing down her face. "And as I already said, Princess

Jory, you are most definitely princess material. I could certainly imagine you in silk and taffeta, velvet and fur, holding a golden scepter."

Jory shook her head. "No, that's not for me, especially the fur thing. I think animals need the fur they were born with more than I do."

Zandar shrugged again. "If you're going to kill the animal, you might as well use all of it. However, if you have a strong objection to fur, you could always go naked."

A tingle shot through Jory at the thought of being naked in front of Zandar. Even more arousing and frightening was the idea of him being naked too. She wondered if he was as large everywhere as his frame suggested, and her core ached with curiosity. Could she handle a man like him? "So I guess the princess is off-limits to anyone who isn't Prince Kendrick?"

He nodded just once, his lips a straight, tight line. "That's correct, Princess Jory."

Feeling braver than she should, Jory stepped a bit closer, lifted her hand, and trailed her fingers down his neck. He swallowed in response, and she gave him a sexy smile similar to the one he'd bestowed up on her earlier. "I guess it's a good thing I'm not Princess Key On Tree then."

"Chiondri." He swallowed again when her fingers dipped a little lower, into the lightweight material of the mesh-like khaki shirt he wore. "You should rest now, and I have things to do."

"What kinds of things?" she asked suggestively. Was she insane to be flirting with this strange man she barely knew? Was man even the right word, considering he came from another planet? It was completely unlike her to be so forthright or open, but then again, rarely had a man stated his interest so plainly, if in a vague fashion.

"You," he said with a growl in his voice that was sexy enough to melt her panties. "If you don't give me space, Princess Jory, I'll be bending you over the nav console in about five minutes. That would be nothing but trouble for both of us, especially if you really are Princess Chiondri.

I don't fancy a death sentence for deflowering the Royal Prince's bride, and I wouldn't think you'd enjoy the punishment for cuckolding the prince either."

Her eyes widened with surprise. "You mean if Chiara sleeps with someone besides the prince...?" She drew her finger across her throat.

He nodded, his expression grim. "That's not the kind of thing most want to risk, is it?"

She shook her head, a surge of disappointment filling her. Unless she could convince Zandar she truly wasn't Chiara, he would never surrender to the attraction simmering between them. That was probably for the best, considering they lived two separate lives on separate ends of the galaxy, but she couldn't deny she was disappointed about never getting to enjoy a tumble with the alien standing near her.

With a sigh, she backed away from him and turned to leave the bridge. "I guess I'll see what the ship has to offer than, Zandar." With an exaggerated sway of her hips, she sashayed from the room and down the direction from which she had come until she was back at the medical bay. Having nothing else to do besides fantasize about the stubborn alien tracker, she decided to have a little nap. Perhaps sleep—or a really sexy dream, complete with orgasm—would banish the ache of desire tingling in her core.

Chapter Three

THE HORRIBLE SOUND of rending metal woke Jory from her nap. A millisecond later, the ship shuddered, and she was thrown from the metal table to the floor, her elbow smashing into the hard tile. With a small cry, she cradled her sore elbow while trying to plant herself securely to keep from tumbling around as the ship shook.

The trembling seemed to go on forever, though it might have just been her perception of events coupled with the confusion of trying to discern what was happening. The ship didn't exactly settle, but it did slow down and stop vibrating enough to allow her to get to her feet. Her elbow was tender, but didn't appear broken, so she gingerly rested it at her side.

As soon as she felt steady enough to walk, Jory stepped slowly, bracing herself for more rumbling to knock her off her feet at any moment, and left the medical bay to head down the corridor. She half-expected Zandar to meet her along the way, but there was no sign of him until she reached the room where she'd found him before. He was busy at the console system, barking orders at the computer and demanding a diagnostic. Her head swam with confusion, and she slowly entered the room, standing near him, but not close enough to distract him. "What's going on, Zandar?"

He cursed—it sounded like a curse anyway, though she didn't recognize his language, of course. Looking frazzled, which was a strange state for the large alien bounty hunter, who always seemed to have everything under control, he looked down at her and shook his head. "Damn ship. The harbinger-class is fast, but can't stand up to anything. If I had my ship, the asteroid would've just bounced off the hull instead of going through."

She scrunched her brow, trying to make sense of his jumbled words and tentatively guessing, "We were hit by an asteroid?"

He nodded as he moved to another section of the ship, with her trailing a few steps behind. "Yes, that's what happened. It was a small one, and the ship's sensors didn't detect it in time to avoid the collision. The proximity alert didn't sound soon enough to take evasive measures, and like I said, the asteroid punched right through the hull."

She swallowed down a bitter surge of nausea, refusing to let the gorge escape. "Are we going to be okay?"

His lack of answer wasn't reassuring, and she tried to tell herself it was because he was focusing on what had happened. They had entered a room that she assumed housed the engine, though she couldn't be sure. There were a lot of metal beams, textured silver walls, and flickering lights with exposed wires, along with a dented area in the semi-transparent wall currently bulging inward. She pointed to the dark mass she could see beyond the wall. "What's that?"

"The asteroid, which finally stopped at the inner hull. The outer hull is completely breached in that section, but the computer was able to engage the airlock in time to keep us from hemorrhaging oxygen."

She arched a brow. "That's a good thing, right?"

Zandar shrugged. "It depends on your definition of good, Princess Jory. We're still alive, but the ansible and the transponder are in that section of the ship."

She frowned. "Ansible and transponder? I don't know what that is. I mean, I kind of know what a transponder is, but only from movies and things back on Earth." It was strange how easily she'd fallen into referring to home as "back on Earth"—and frightening how far away her planet seemed at the moment.

"An ansible is used for long-range communications, and it's a crucial part of the ship. We can send out short-range messages with the computer system, but without an ansible, we're nowhere near where we need to be in order to be within range to send or receive messages from Gentarres."

She didn't need an elaborate, technical explanation to work out that was bad. "And the transponder?"

He looked grim. "It's like a GPS unit, though that's simplified, of course. It allows the Gentarrens to track the ship. With the last coordinates they received before the asteroid destroyed the transponder, they'll know vaguely where we are in the quadrant, but not exactly where we ended up."

"Ended up?" Jory shook her head, her mind awhirl with confusion. "I don't understand. That sounds like we aren't going to be here."

"That's exactly what it means, Princess. The ship won't be capable of flight for much longer. We've already dropped out of iono-space, and I'm doing my best, along with the computer's help, to keep this hunk of junk together until we find a place to land."

"You mean like a friendly planet where we can get some help?" she asked hopefully, knowing it was ridiculously Pollyannaish of her to expect that outcome.

He laughed, and it was a harsh bark that held little amusement. "No, *lyndrahna*, I mean the kind of planet where we're lucky to survive the conditions, and where we can wait for the rescue party. If we're lucky, the computer can identify an Exeter planet—meaning roughly habitable—that will give us a chance of actually surviving."

"And if we're unlucky?" Her stomach dipped with anxiety as she awaited his answer, though she already knew before he even spoke again.

"We crash, explode, or implode if the hull breach gets any worse."

She shook her head, refusing to believe what she was hearing. "This is officially, absolutely, completely the worst day ever." She glared at him. "I should be home right now holding my cat and trying to find a new job instead of worrying about surviving a spaceship crash. What are you going to do about this?"

He shrugged. "You assume I can do anything, princess. We'll either crash land and survive—or die during the crash—or explode before we get the chance to set down somewhere."

"How can you be so calm about the whole thing? Aren't you even a little bit alarmed that we're going to die?"

Zandar nodded, but looked resolved. "Of course, but panicking won't change the outcome."

She gnashed her teeth, frustrated with his equanimity. Jory wanted to scream and run around in a frenzy, and she would have felt just a bit better if he'd joined her in that pointless, though cathartic, venture. An alarm suddenly sounded, and she yelped. "What's that? Are we dying? Is the ship about to crash or explode?"

"No, that's the klaxon alerting us the ship has found somewhere for us to land."

She practically ran to keep up with the pace he set as he strode back to the navigation system. "Do you know if it's a safe planet?"

"I had the computer search for parameters that would include anything with even the lowest probability of survivability, so we have a better chance on whatever planet the computer has found then we do just waiting for this heap of junk to fall apart."

"That's not very reassuring, Zandar."

"Sorry, Princess Jory, but I'm not really the reassuring type." He spoke brusquely, but gave her a tiny smile.

Jory peered over his shoulder as he sat down in front of the nav console. A strange alien language flashed across the screen, and she leaned closer to see it, though of course she couldn't decipher the meaning.

An image appeared to the right of his elbow, and it looked like a barren wasteland. They were still far away from the planet, but close enough the computer could provide some sketchy details of the planet's topography. She didn't see patches of blue to indicate water, but didn't know if that was how water would really look from orbit anyway. Her sole experience was based on media and movies from Earth. "Is that a desert?"

"It appears to be."

"Are we going to survive?"

Zandar looked up at her over his shoulder, his tail absently wrapping around the back of his chair and brushing her arm, perhaps in a gesture of comfort but more likely an accident. He didn't seem like the nurturing type who would expend energy reassuring her when there wasn't actually reassurance to offer. Still, he didn't have to be so blunt, she decided with a glare, when he answered her.

"We're about to find out, Princess Jory."

Chapter Four

IT WAS HOT. THE KIND of hot she'd never experienced before, and as a teen, Jory had spent two weeks in midsummer with her grandmother in Arizona, enduring hundred and twenty-degree days when her grandmother refused to turn on the air conditioner because of the expense.

Remnants of the ship that had survived the crash provided some shelter, and she was surprised to find the semitransparent metal was sturdier than she would have imagined. A big chunk of the ship was missing, allowing the heat from the outside to permeate the interior, though the vessel appeared to be maintaining its environmental controls.

She wondered if there was enough oxygen content in the planet's air to allow them to breathe comfortably, or if it was something the ship was doing to provide or stabilize the oxygen levels. That she could even think about that without a hysterical giggle amazed her. She had never been a science fiction fan, other than the occasional movie and a girl-crush on Sigourney Weaver as Ripley. Unfortunately, Jory was nothing like Ripley, and she was completely out of her element.

Two days had passed since the ship had crashed onto the strange, hot planet. She had no idea how to measure exactly how much time had passed on Earth, but the two suns had risen and set in the time that they had been here. During that time, Zandar had not awakened. He bore a deep cut on his temple, and she had muddled through trying to close it up by using supplies in the medical bay. Since half of them had been unfamiliar, she had done her best to guess their intended purposes.

He had a clumsy-looking bandage on the wound that consisted of some kind of gossamer wrap. She'd assumed it was a bandage, but for all she knew, it could be an alien maxi pad. That idea made her want to giggle too, but she resisted the urge. The fact that she was constantly on the verge of laughing wasn't a good sign. It meant she was in panic mode, and the slightest little thing could tip her over completely.

Surprisingly, she had survived the crash unscathed, save for a cut along her arm. It had bled for a few minutes before stopping, so she hadn't worried about it. Instead, she had focused all her attention on the massive alien who had kidnapped her and whose fault it was they were stranded on this desert planet with no communication.

Not that she hadn't tried. Jory had done her best to figure out the computer console and all the different systems, hampered by her lack of ability to speak or read his alien language. The computer continually beeped quietly in the background, interspersed with an occasional shrill alarm she assumed was not an indicator of something good to come. Without the knowledge to determine the problem, and without Zandar awake to look into it, she was left struggling in the dark, figuratively.

The environmental controls and the ship still worked well enough to provide lighting, food, and water. Thankfully, whoever had designed the sustenance systems had the forethought to include visual instructions, so she had been able to glean how to get water out of the dispenser and food from the machine. She refused to use the "Star Trek" word for that—mainly because she couldn't remember what the show had called it.

The food was strange, but not the worst thing she'd ever eaten. A solid lump of blue-green that resembled algae, it was difficult to feed to someone who was unconscious, so she worried about Zandar, who had not been awake enough to eat anything. Afraid of making him choke, she had satisfied herself with only dabbing at his lips with a moist cloth and occasionally running her fingertips dipped in water inside his lips. It was an intimate gesture, but she was too concerned about him to get an illicit thrill. Okay, much of an illicit thrill.

Jory didn't pretend she hadn't sneaked more than one or two long looks at his sexy body underneath the ripped khaki mesh coverall-thing he wore, and she had touched him a bit more than necessary to tend to his wounds, but she had not crossed any inappropriate lines.

She might be sexually frustrated, but she wasn't the type of woman to violate a man when he was vulnerable and naked. Not that he was naked. His mesh thing still covered him mostly, but it had ripped down the chest and one shoulder, revealing a solidly muscled magenta chest with just a sprinkling of silvery hair.

Thinking of his head reminded her it was time to check the dressing again, and Jory crouched over him to carefully peel back the bandage. The wound still looked fearsome, but it had started to crust over. There was no more of the strange purplish-blue blood leaking from the wound, and she assumed that was a good sign. Carefully, she returned the bandage, which immediately adhered to his skin by some mechanism of its own. Still leaning over him, she stretched across to reach for the cup of water and yelped when his arms came around her. "Zandar, are you awake?"

He made some sort of groaning, grumbling sound as he turned over, taking her with him. Jory ended up trapped under his bulky frame, one of his hands confining her wrists above her head. Her body couldn't help responding to his proximity, even as concern overrode desire. His eyes were still half-mast and didn't seem completely alert. "Zandar, can you hear me?"

"Female," he grunted. Or at least that's what it sounded like.

Jory tried to shove him off, but Zandar maintained his hold on her easily. She gasped when his mouth moved to her cheek, and he licked her before moving lower to nibble on her neck. Her nerve endings sparked to life, and she writhed underneath him even as she tried to resist the urge to respond.

It was obvious he had no idea what he was doing, or perhaps even who she was. Since he had been so concerned about deflowering

Princess Chiondri, she didn't think he would easily surrender to desire if he were alert. Allowing him to continue would be akin to taking advantage of him, wouldn't it?

As she tried to push him away, Jory realized there was no *allowed* about it. Zandar wasn't moving, and she didn't see how she could stop him. If she felt threatened or reluctant, she would have been terrified under the circumstances. Instead, she couldn't help melting against him as his mouth moved from her neck to her lips, and he took hers in a deep kiss.

This was what she'd been wanting since almost the moment she'd seen the fierce warrior, and though her conscience niggled, Jory didn't try to stop him again as his tongue swept inside her mouth, and she sucked on his while stroking it with her own. He tasted vaguely metallic, and while not unpleasant, was certainly strange. She wondered if it was his typical taste, or perhaps a side effect of dehydration or even all the bleeding he had done from the head wound.

Abruptly remembering just how seriously he was injured, Jory forced herself to do the right thing. She pressed her palms to his chest and shoved as hard as she could, managing to move him a few inches. He seemed dazed, and somehow she managed to turn him onto his back and scramble away before he could grab her again.

He wore a scowl of displeasure, but soon slipped back into unconsciousness. Jory shook her head at her own loss of self-control. She had almost allowed him to do something he wouldn't when he was alert, and she knew what kind of physical shape he was in presently. Sex with her literally might have killed him.

Perhaps it might've killed her too, though she suspected from pleasure rather than pain or injury. With a sigh of regret, and the cold comfort of knowing she had followed her conscience and done the responsible thing, Jory turned her attention to coaxing dinner from the computer and waited for Zandar to awaken.

IT WAS SEVERAL HOURS later before he moved again, and this time, his eyes opened fully. She could tell a difference immediately by the alertness in his expression. "Zandar, can you hear me?"

He blinked his eyes, drawing attention to the fact that the vibrant purple had faded slightly. She frowned with concern. "Zandar, can you please answer me?"

"Yes, Princess Jory." He groaned and grabbed his head as he spoke, clearly in pain from the simple motion.

She scooted closer, leaning over the bounty hunter to peer into his eyes. She had a very basic understanding of human first-aid, and she hoped some of the principles applied to Zandar, since they had similar physiology. His pupils were the same size, which she took as a good sign. "Where does it hurt?" she asked softly, not wanting to aggravate his aching head.

"Everywhere," he rasped.

She believed that. He had gotten quite banged up during the crash landing, mainly because he had insisted on covering her body with his own and protecting her. She had protested, not wanting to be a damsel-in-distress, but his insistence on protection had touched her.

She'd tried not to allow the sour thought to take hold that perhaps he was guarding his bounty, whom he believed to be the future princess of Gentarres, rather than her personally. Instead, she'd chosen to believe it was because he liked and desired her with the same intensity she felt for him. The kiss from earlier seemed indicative of that, but she couldn't bring it up without an awkward conversation.

"I need *Ohdahan*."

She frowned at him. "Oh Da Han?" She repeated slowly. "Who is that? As far as I can tell, there's no way to communicate. I haven't been able to figure it out anyway, though I guess that isn't saying much, since I've never been good with that sort of thing."

He shook his head, and then groaned again, clearly regretting the movement. "*Ohdahan* is a medication that relieves pain. Silver tube, green mist."

With a nod she imagined he probably didn't see, since his eyes were closed again, she got to her feet. A glance at him revealed he'd placed his forearm across them as though blocking out the light that was slowly seeping away with the second sun disappearing under the horizon

With a mission in mind, Jory strode to what was left of the medical bay. It was in complete disarray, just like the rest of the ship, so it took her a while to locate anything resembling his description of *Ohdahan*. Eventually, she found a spilled drawer full of silver tubes, and the next challenge was figuring out which one was the right medication.

No, she supposed the next challenge was actually discovering how to use the silver tube so she could test the mist inside. It was a long cylinder with no obvious buttons, and she looked at it for several minutes, trying to discern what it did or how it worked. With no answer forthcoming, and recalling the biometric panels on the doors of the spacecraft, she scooped up all the tubes she could find, which numbered eleven, and returned to her temporary patient.

Zandar slept again, though he didn't seem quite so deeply asleep this time. This seemed to be more of a healing slumber than one verging on the edge of death.

With an air of experimentation, she lifted his hand and placed one of the tubes in his palm, wrapping his fingers around it with her own on the outside. Within a millisecond, the little tube came to life, and a bar with a flashing indicator appeared on the side.

It was tricky to use his other thumb to swipe the bar, but she managed. As the red indicator lights moved downward in one smooth motion under his thumb, a lemon-yellow mist emerged from the tube. She immediately released the dispensing mechanism and set aside the tube. It wasn't the same shade of sickly yellow he had used to gas her, so she didn't want to waste it in case it was something valuable.

She tested three more tubes before finding one that emitted a green mist. As she examined it, she decided the most logical way to administer it would be into his face. She didn't know if she should stick it in his mouth or his nose, so she brought the tube as close as she could, centered halfway between both.

With some cursing and a bit of contortionism she hadn't known she could perform, she managed to hold the tube with one of his hands and dispense the mist with his thumb from the other hand. Nothing happened for a few minutes, and she set aside the tube carefully, keeping it segregated from the others she had not yet explored, and the pile she knew weren't *Ohdahan*.

Slowly, Zandar's breathing relaxed further, no longer sounding rough, and his muscles seemed to loosen. He was clearly more at ease, and she wasn't surprised when his eyes opened about an hour later.

This time, they were the same vibrant purple they had been before, and his awareness seemed to be at its previous level before the accident. He touched his head gingerly, but without the obvious pain from before. "You found the *Ohdahan*," he said, sounding satisfied.

She nodded, waving toward the silver tubes. "There were several in the medical bay, but I don't know what any of them do. I thought maybe something else might help you."

He nodded, looking impressed as he glanced at her. "If you are truly an Earth woman and don't understand our technology, it is a most impressive feat to be able to discern how these tubes worked. If you aren't being deceptive with me, Princess Jory, I likely owe you my life."

She didn't know whether to be pleased by the praise or annoyed by the slight hint of accusation. "I am from Earth, I'm not Princess Chiondri, and believe it or not, I'm not a complete moron. I assumed since several of the doors work with biometrics, it was feasible the medicine might do the same. Since I'm not your species, I used your hands to see if it would work, and it did. You don't owe me your life, though if it will make you more inclined to take me home, I'll happily accept that debt."

He laughed softly, barely touching his head as though chasing a tiny wave of pain. "At this point in time, Jory, I would be happy to take you home if I could. First, I must determine the state of the ship."

Jory put up a hand. "Actually, shouldn't you check the medicine to see if there's anything else that can help you?"

"Yes, I suppose that would be sensible." He took the tubes she extended, obviously knowing what they were by some means as he sorted through them. Finally, he lifted a tube and inserted it into his mouth. Dark blue mist emerged before he closed his lips around it and inhaled deeply.

"What was that?"

"*Hindafor*. It's good for internal injuries and will heal any puncture wounds or torn internal organs. It also accelerates cellular repair."

"Okay." She pointed toward his forehead, where what she hoped was a bandage was still in place. "Does that mean your cut will magically disappear?"

He half-rolled his eyes. "There's nothing magical about our technology, Jory. We're just more advanced than Earth. And in answer to your question, no, it won't magically heal, but it will speed up recovery, and I'll likely have no sign of the injury within a couple of days."

She was impressed by the speed of that, but decided not to tell him since he was already being an arrogant prick about his technology versus hers. "Now what do we do with the ship?"

"First I'll try to see if the transponder or ansible will work."

Jory was already shaking her head. "There's no point, Zandar. If they're where you said earlier, that part of the ship's gone. I don't know if it's on the planet or if it was destroyed during the crash, or even during entry into the atmosphere." Wow, she sounded just like one of those heroines in a science fiction movie, as though she actually knew what the hell she was talking about.

"I see." He said something harsh, but softly, that she assumed was a curse word in his language. "The next step is to run a diagnostic on the ship to see what still works and what doesn't."

"That makes sense. I tried to figure out the systems, but I don't speak the language or read it, and I had no idea what I was doing." Her face flushed as she admitted, "Honestly, I can barely program the Hopper on my satellite box."

He seemed confused by that, but didn't ask questions, for which she was grateful. Jory had no idea how she would explain what a satellite box or the Hopper were, other than a very basic definition. Of course, with his so-superior alien technology, he would probably immediately grasp it and be sure to tell her how they had improved upon that too.

Resisting the urge to roll her eyes, she said, "The food and water things still seem to be working, and I guess the computer is maintaining some kind of environmental control, because while it's hot in here, it appears to be much hotter outside."

Suddenly, his gaze dropped from her eyes to her chest, Jory abruptly remembered she had removed everything but her camisole and panties more than a day ago. It had been so hot in the ship and with him completely unconscious at the time, she had decided there was no harm in a little less modesty.

Technically, she had worn less to the beach, so she shouldn't feel so self-conscious—especially since he had made her strip to this point before to check for the biochip. Still, she couldn't deny things had changed, probably because of the kiss they had shared. She supposed *shared* wasn't the right word, since he had no memory of it, and with that heated look in his eyes, it wasn't wise to tell him about it now.

Or ever. Yes, never sounded like the perfect amount of time to allow between the kissing and admitting they had done so.

The longer he stared at her, the more her blood heated, especially when she saw how his purple eyes darkened as he became aroused. He was much more alert than he had been earlier, so she didn't think it would be detrimental to his health if they indulged in their desires. However, as he leaned nearer with her straining to meet him, that annoying alarm she had almost gotten used to over the past couple of days sounded again. Jory cursed quietly as he got to his feet in a single bound.

"You move pretty fast for someone with a head injury," she said, trying not to sound disgruntled. She was happy he was mobile again, but the klaxon had been an unwelcome distraction, leaving her grumpy and frustrated.

He ignored her observation as he turned from the area where she had set up temporary shelter, clearly in search of the part of the ship from which the alarm emanated. Without awaiting an invitation, Jory stood up and followed behind him.

He led her down what was left of the hallway, and they both winced each time they encountered an area where heat from the outside seemed to seep in through cracks or missing chunks of the wall. "This is one hell of a hot planet," said Zandar.

Jory nodded, grateful once again for the fact the ship had held together at least enough to provide shelter. He moved so quickly she had a little trouble keeping up with her shorter legs, but she didn't ask him to slow down. Despite it having interrupted their moment, she was as eager as he was to know what was causing the alarm to sound periodically.

He went to the nav console, his fingers flying over the flashing buttons, and he spoke something guttural to the computer. Within a couple of moments, data flashed across the screen, and the more he read, the darker his expression became.

She was hesitant to ask, but had never been one to shy away from knowing the truth. "What is it? Is it bad, Zandar?"

He took a deep breath before he turned back to her, his expression calm, but the set of his shoulders indicated repressed tension. "It could be bad, Princess Jory. We have a radiation leak in the ion generator, but so far, the shield is keeping it from leaking outside the containment area."

Her stomach tightened with fear, and she attempted a lighthearted tone that fell flat. "Are we going to be glowing in the dark soon?"

"No, the computer will warn us before it gets to that point." He must have seen her flash of alarm, because he held up his hands. "Relax, Jory. It might not reach that stage. We should be rescued before we have to worry about radiation compromising the containment system."

She tilted her head slightly to the side, trying to remember anything she'd ever heard about radiation. "Doesn't radiation scramble electronics or something?"

"High enough and prolonged levels of radiation could interfere with electronics, but the containment system is hardened and the ship's alarm is on a separate configuration with built-in redundancies. Even if the shield fails, whether from radiation or structural damage, the ship will let us know before it reaches a critical stage."

She turned slightly to look out the semitransparent wall to the desert beyond, which didn't look any more hospitable even at sunset than it did during the hottest part of the day, with both suns directly overhead. "If we have to leave the ship, we'll die out there."

"It's possible, but I know a thing or two about desert survival, Princess Jory. Trust me. I'll do my best to get you to Gentarres and Prince Kendrick." He winked at her.

She snorted. "I can hardly wait for that, Zandar." She turned back to him, her gaze locking with his. "You know I'm not Chiara. Why do you keep up the pretense?"

"I don't know for sure that you aren't the princess." He crossed his arms over his chest, giving her a stern look. "Until I know that, I can't act any other way."

"What does it matter? We're going to die anyway. Might as well entertain ourselves in the meantime." She stopped speaking, eyes wide at her own boldness. She had certainly asked previous lovers for sex, but had never propositioned an alien bounty hunter within a few days of meeting—especially not one who had dragged her to the middle of nowhere and crash landed her on a desert planet.

He arched a brow, his expression indicating his interest, even as he shook his head. "I can't do that. Your virginity has to be preserved for the prince if you are Princess Chiondri."

"So you're basically a virginity babysitter." She snorted again. "I bet you're sorry you took this job, aren't you, Zandar?" She had a sense of satisfaction that he was just as miserable with the setup as she was, though he didn't have the added injustice of having his very identity questioned, or having a proposition for sex tossed back at him, albeit politely.

The corner of his mouth curled upward, and he inclined his head a bit. "I'll concede you might be more trouble than you're worth, Princess Jory."

"They can't be paying you enough for this one." She tipped her head as she speculated on the affixed value of a runaway princess. "What are they paying you for this job?"

He shifted slightly on his feet, looking discomforted. "There is no monetary compensation."

She shook her head. "You aren't even being paid to retrieve me...Chiondri, I mean? That's not really fair, is it?"

"It's complicated and has to do with familial obligations."

She nodded. "Oh, that's right. I forgot your father was a Gentile bairn."

His lips twitched. "I know very well you can say it properly, Princess Jory. Your game grows old."

She grinned at him. "Does it really? Then why do you have trouble not laughing every time I deliberately mispronounce your home world?"

His expression turned cool. "It's not my home world, remember? I'm from Karadis first."

She nodded, determined to avoid anything that would be a sore subject and send him into a foul mood. Instead, she decided to take pity on him. "Are you hungry? There's some strange food that comes out of that machine-thingy. I can make us something."

He nodded, his expression one of interest. "I could eat."

Chapter Five

AFTER DINNER, WHEN Zandar showed her the proper way to work the machine to produce a far tastier meal than her previous attempts, he seemed tired again. They retired to the sleeping space, and she tried to hide her awkwardness.

Until then, she had just lain beside the unconscious alien, telling herself she had to be near if he needed assistance. Now that he was awake and alert, there was no reason to lie on the makeshift bed with him. "I think I'll go to the medical bay to see if I can scavenge more bedding."

"That won't be necessary, Princess Jory."

She waved to the bed, which had been fine when he wasn't aware of her presence, but would be a tight fit for two people who weren't well acquainted or planned to become that way. "Really, there's no room now that you're awake."

His lips twitched. "I won't be awake for long, so you might as well sleep beside me. At least that way I know you won't be escaping and forcing me to track you down again."

She rolled her eyes, even as she moved closer to him. "Only an idiot would go into that desert, and you should know by now I'm not an idiot—and I'm not Princess Chiondri."

She gave a small nod to emphasize her point as she dropped down to the floor, self-conscious of the position and the way it accentuated the roundness of her booty. As she glanced to the side, she saw Zandar admiring her bum with a gleam of appreciation, and the self-consciousness fled. Apparently, he was a man who liked a well-rounded set of cheeks.

She scooted over to the edge as much as she could when Zandar prepared to lie down beside her. She could see his pain was returning, so she rifled through tubes of medicine until she found *Ohdahan* again. As he lay down beside her with a small groan, she extended the silver tube. "Can you have more of this yet?"

He took the tube and nodded. "I can, but it's a bit strong for my current pain levels. Would you hand me the other tubes?"

Jory passed over the shallow tray and watched him sort through them by whatever method he used to identify the medications, until he pulled one from the pile and inserted it in his mouth. He inhaled an orange mist before handing the tube to her. "That should provide enough pain relief, but it will make me sleep heavily."

She laughed. "You've done nothing but sleep heavy the last couple of days, Zandar. I'm used to that." Abruptly, she stopped speaking as she remembered the kiss that had taken place earlier in the day, the one she had barely escaped—not because he'd held her against her will, but because she hadn't wanted it to end. "Does it lower your inhibitions?" she asked with forced casualness.

He arched a brow. "Nothing lowers my inhibitions, Princess Jory."

She barely bit back a giggle at the knowledge he was wrong about his own perceived mental strength. Still, enlightening him would mean admitting to the kiss and her reluctance to end it. She settled for a small nod as she lay down on the bedding, which did little to hide the fact they were sleeping on top of a hard metal surface. Jory groaned and grunted as she turned and tried to get comfortable a few times before she heard Zandar let out a loud sigh.

As Jory started to inquire about his state of health, she yelped instead when his arms were suddenly around her, pulling her atop his massive frame. Though he was hard and muscled, he was far more comfortable than the floor covered by thin blankets. She offered a token resistance. "I shouldn't do this, because you're injured."

"I will never be too injured to hold you, Jory." He groaned as she shifted, but it wasn't a sound of pain. "I only wish I could do more," he muttered almost too quietly to hear.

It didn't take long for Jory to realize what he meant, as her thigh pressed into the hard length of his erection growing against her skin. Her panties dampened just at the thought of being so near him in a state of arousal, and it was all she could do not to keep squirming in search of relief. This was a special kind of torture, even worse than being stranded on a desert planet after being kidnapped by an alien.

"Good night, Princess Jory."

"Good night, Zandar." To her surprise, she was already falling asleep. She hadn't rested well the past couple of nights as she had watched over Zandar, but she'd expected to be too keyed up to sleep on top of the alien, especially with her body craving his. Instead, her eyes closed, and she curled against him, deciding maybe all the rest of the things she had been through were worth it just to have this moment with Zandar.

SOMETIME IN THE MIDDLE of the night, their positions had shifted, and Jory woke to a heavy weight atop her. Slowly, her eyes opened and awareness returned along with the realization she was pinned under Zandar, who slept deeply. It was nice having his weight on her, but parts of her body were going numb. He was too much for her to fully support, but she was reluctant to wake him, knowing he would immediately move away from her. "Zandar, are you awake?" she whispered softly, half-hoping he wouldn't rouse.

His answer was a quiet snore, so she attempted to shift underneath him to relieve some of the more uncomfortable pressure points. Changing position alleviated her discomfort, but fueled her arousal.

She had fallen asleep easily, but dreams had followed her into slumber, and the rest she had gotten had been punctuated with naughty images for the duration. Looking at the semitransparent wall, the suns were already rising, and the nighttime didn't seem to last as long here as it did on Earth. Perhaps that was because of the two suns?

Jory touched his face, brushing her fingers across his lips and hoping to coax him awake. "Zandar? You need to turn over."

He awakened slightly, but instead of turning, he wrapped her in his arms and pulled her closer as his mouth nuzzled her neck. Jory knew she should push him away or try harder to wake him fully, but she allowed herself to enjoy a moment of sensual pleasure.

His large palms grasped her buttocks and lifted her more firmly against him, and she whimpered with need when he grinded his cock against her heated folds. If it weren't for their layers of clothing, which were few and thin, they would be lovers right now. She couldn't resist arching against him and circling her hips as his erection pressed more firmly into her, barely deterred by the lace of her panties.

Her heart raced with excitement, and she clutched his shoulders as she arched against him, lost to sensation that overrode common sense. Jory turned her head, forcing his face away from her neck so she could capture his lips in a deep kiss. He ravaged her mouth, and she enjoyed every second, stroking his tongue with her own and straining to meet him.

His tail tickled her shoulder, and she started at the sensation, having completely forgotten about it for a moment. It must have been an autonomic response, because he was still unconscious. As the tail stroked her skin, she relished the taste of his mouth, which still had a faintly metallic taste, though not as pronounced.

He tensed suddenly, and it was obvious he had fully awakened. In a desperate attempt to keep him from leaving, or doing what he considered the right thing, Jory wrapped her thighs around his hips and tightened her arms around his back. She increased the fervor of the kiss, and he hesitated for only a second before resuming the embrace.

His large hands cupped her face, making her feel tiny and delicate as he devoured her mouth like a starving man. She was feeling equally needy and was still writhing beneath him through the clothes. When he moved his head slightly, she dragged in a deep breath to compensate for the fuzzyheaded feeling that had swept over her while they kissed so passionately. She hadn't noticed the lack of oxygen then, and she didn't care too much about it now.

"We can't," he said in a thick voice that sounded like he was being tortured.

"We can. I promise I'm not Princess Chiondri, so please don't deny us both what we want, Zandar. We might not even get off this planet, so what does it matter?"

"You make it difficult to do the right thing." He growled the accusation as he grasped a handful of her hair and dragged her head backward, exposing her neck. A second later, his lips moved over the delicate column of flesh, alternating between nibbling and licking.

One of his hands moved to her breast, and while she was generously endowed, his hand was more than adequate to cover the full globe. His thumb stroked across her nipple, and she cried out as she continued thrusting against his cock, though it was still sheathed by his clothing.

As he kissed her throat and rubbed her breast, his other hand still held her hair in a grasp that was slightly painful, but only served to enhance her pleasure as it reminded her how desperately he wanted her. His tail wrapped around her stomach in a loving caress, and it didn't seem all that strange while lost in the haze of passion.

She couldn't stop thrusting against him rapidly, her mind having no control over her body's actions. To her amazement, she hovered on the edge of orgasm, and as he pushed his hips firmly forward, pressing his cock against her pussy as hard as he could, she came with a loud shout of satisfaction. It had been many years since she had dry-humped her way to an orgasm, and not since she had become fully sexually active.

The release relaxed her slightly, but didn't blunt the hunger for the large alien. Jory pulled at his clothes, struggling to get him out of the mesh suit. "This thing is a pain in the..." She trailed off as she tried to work the fabric down his body. In her frustration, she tugged forcefully while considering tearing at it with her teeth.

"It's amazingly durable body armor, and I doubt you'll be able to rip it off with your bare hands, Princess Jory." A strong note of humor underlay the words.

"Don't underestimate how much I want to see you naked, Zandar, and how much I want that hard cock inside me."

He growled low in his throat and was on his feet in less than a second. Jory watched with appreciation as he stripped out of the mesh with economical movements she couldn't have mirrored on her own. In what seemed like no time at all, he was naked and returned to her. Jory helped him pull off her camisole, and before she could assist him with removing her panties, Zandar had torn the fragile lace.

She groaned, regretting the loss of her only pair, but it was a fleeting thought as his fingers parted her folds, their size easily finding all of her sensitive spots seemingly at once. He stroked her clit as his fingers pressed gently into her sheath, unerringly finding her g-spot. She wondered if she shared similar physiology to the females of his species, or if he was just that good.

"Please, Zandar, I've already come once. Just take me."

He shook his head, though perspiration beaded his forehead. "I can't do that, Princess Jory."

She gritted her teeth. "Are you kidding me? I thought we were past that nonsense. I am not Chiondri."

He grinned slightly, though it appeared more of a grimace of pain. Perhaps he was having a difficult time holding back. "I believe you, Jory, but there's a difference in our physiology. A marked difference, and I don't want to hurt you when I make love you to you for the first time."

Her eyes widened with a mixture of apprehension and anticipation, and she pushed him away so she could get a good look at the erection awaiting her. Jory's eyes widened as she saw the girth and length of his cock. It was a smoothly rounded tower, and the magenta was a darker shade than the rest of his body. Was that the blood flow from arousal, or was his cock naturally darker than the rest of his body? She filed away the question to ask later as she reached for him. When she wrapped her hand around his length, her fingers wouldn't meet.

She swallowed a lump in her throat as she stroked him slowly. His erection swelled even larger, and she let go with a small smile. "I see your point." Lying back, she surrendered to his fingers as he rubbed and stretched her to accept him. Apparently, he must have decided she was ready somewhere in the midst of her third orgasm, because he knelt between her thighs.

Struggling not to tense up, she breathed deeply as the head nudged her channel. Her eyes widened when he pushed slowly inside her, but she accepted him much more easily than she had anticipated. Jory moaned as Zandar gave her his full length after moving at a torturously slow pace.

"So tight." He grasped her hair again in that primitive way that was such a turn-on, because it revealed his precarious control. "Mine," he grunted as he withdrew before surging deeply inside her again.

"Yours," she whispered, completely surrendering to the overly-filled sensation between her thighs. He had ruined her for Earth men, but she couldn't summon the energy to care. It was worth never again having his equal—figuratively or literally—to experience this moment with her sexy alien.

In addition to being generously endowed, Zandar also had incredible stamina. She lost track of how long they made love, or how many orgasms she had. When he finally stiffened inside her before his cock twitched, she came again. Warm splashes of his release painted her insides as he collapsed atop her, his arms shaking with the effort to hold himself above her.

As one, they rolled onto their sides, still cuddled together. Discreetly, she reached for a bandage and used it as a makeshift cloth for cleaning up. Her eyes widened with surprise when she saw his purple-blue semen with iridescent streaks. Even his cum was interstellar, she thought with a barely suppressed grin.

"How are you?" he asked, his voice a bit gruff.

"Mmm, I'm fine." She laid her head on his chest and placed her hand across his stomach. "That was amazing."

"Yes, it was, Princess Jory." He pulled her even closer. "Rest now so we can do it again."

THEY SPENT THE NEXT two days carrying on like a couple of honeymooners, doing little besides eating, sleeping, and having sex. Jory swore his essence was addictive, because the more she had, the more she wanted. She seemed to have a similar effect on him, but he had a bit more self-control.

Zandar refused to let them stay in bed the entire time. Instead, he focused some of their attention on preparing for survival, both inside and out of the ship. He scouted the exterior of the planet one morning, discovering there was enough oxygen in the planet's atmosphere to meet both their needs. He also inventoried their supplies and insisted they organize them and prepare bug-out packs.

On the third evening after he had awakened from his pseudo-coma, the shrill alarm started again. This time, it didn't stop after a few minutes. Instead, the volume escalated and continued without pause.

She didn't have to ask what it meant, and she hurried to find her clothes. Her panties were a completely lost cause, and she dreaded the idea of wearing the skirt and jacket, but she shoved it into the pack Zandar had helped her prepare two days before. "I'm scared," she said softly as she slipped on the skirt over her camisole.

"I know, but I'll do my best to keep you safe." He passed her a section of bandage.

She took it and started to put it in her pack, assuming he wanted a first-aid kit, though she'd sworn he'd already packed that in his heavier bag. His hand on hers had her pausing, and she looked up at him with a question in her eyes.

"Wrap it around your feet. Your shoes are useless, and the bandage will adhere to your skin for at least a few days."

She nodded, fashioning a clumsy pair of makeshift shoes from the strange bandage material. Once it formed to her feet, the bumps seemed to smooth out, and she groaned with pleasure. "My god, I'm going to reverse engineer this stuff, patent it, and run Dr. Scholl's out of business when I get back to Earth."

He laughed softly. "I understood a bit of that, Jory—enough to know it will be beyond your capabilities."

She rolled her eyes, allowing him to distract her from her fear as they collected a few more necessities while moving through the broken ship. "Yes, I know. Earthlings are primitive."

Zandar laughed again. "Somewhat, but I meant you specifically. You can't program your hopping device, so how can you reverse engineer something?"

Her smartass retort disappeared as they neared a wide opening in the ship. This would clearly be their escape hatch. "Do we really have to do this, Zandar?"

He took her hand, squeezing reassuringly. "I'm afraid we must."

She had the craziest urge to tell him she loved him, though that couldn't be true. She barely knew Zandar beyond a physical level. It had to be fear and the passionate closeness they had indulged in the past few days. Instead, she settled for squeezing his hand and taking a step with him out of the ship and onto the planet.

Death seemed inevitable out here in this blistering wasteland, but it was guaranteed if they stayed on the ship. She did her best to keep pace with him as they rushed away from the wreckage. Jory assumed they had to make a minimum safe distance before the shields collapsed, or it wouldn't matter that they had abandoned the site.

PRINCESS BY MISTAKE

Chapter Six

IT WAS SO HOT SHE COULD barely breathe, let alone think. Jory suspected she was relying too much on Zandar to get her through. He was practically carrying her, and she knew it wasn't fair, but she couldn't channel her inner Ripley. Either she'd never had one, or that part of her had died of hyperthermia hours ago.

At some point, he stopped and let her rest under a shelter he erected. It was a clever little cube that popped up into a lightweight square made from the same semitransparent metal as the ship's walls. She guzzled the water he offered, though she thought about asking if they should conserve it. She didn't, because she knew his answer would be yes, and she didn't have it in her to be sensible at the moment.

After a bit of rest, she was more aware and leaned closer to him to view his wristband. His tail flicked lazily near her face, providing a small bit of airflow for which she was grateful. "What do you see?"

"The containment system failed about two hours ago."

She frowned. "Are we far enough away?"

"Yes, *lyndrahna*. Radiation won't harm us now."

"Just this planet," she said with a soft sigh. Tilting her head, she asked, "What does *lyndrahna* mean? You've used it a few times, and I keep forgetting to ask."

His brow furrowed. "I suppose the literal translation would be 'one with a succulent gluteal muscle,' but its intended meaning is an endearment and closest to the English equivalent of 'sweetcheeks.'"

She giggled. "I guess the people of Karadis have mastered the art of romance." It felt good to laugh after the stressful day trekking through the dessert. "What will we do now, Zandar?"

"We'll rest during the hottest part of the day and resume walking tonight."

She frowned. "Why? What are we walking toward, Zandar?"

He pointed to an amber ragged-edged circle on the three-dimensional schematic projecting from his wristband. "I can't be sure, but I believe this is an underground lake. If so, it might solve our water shortage."

She swallowed, suddenly guilty about the amount of water she'd drunk. "How critical are our water problems?"

"We have enough for about three days. There's a portable water concentrator in my pack, but the humidity in the air is almost nonexistent, so it would take much too long to extract and convert it."

She laid her head on his thigh, not verbalizing yet again that they were going to die. They both knew it, but the constant reminder would accomplish nothing. Jory shifted on the semitransparent metal to allow Zandar to lie down beside her. They should eat something, but she was too tired, and he must have been too. Instead, they slept.

Loud noises woke her, and she sat up abruptly, tensing as Zandar held her against his body. "What is it?" she whispered.

"I don't know." He gestured toward one of the semi-translucent walls. "I saw movement and heard noises, but it's too dark to make out anything."

They didn't have to speculate long. Suddenly, the noises took on a strangely familiar sound, somewhere between a shrill hoot and a harsh screech. Jory realized it wasn't the sounds themselves that were familiar. Instead, it was the pattern—one of rhythmically repeated reverberations that suggested speech. Or a chant.

A war chant? She clutched Zandar as the voices grew closer, swelling in intensity. As she waited to learn their fate, she wondered if they might have been better off staying at the ship and surrendering to that end instead.

Chapter Seven

JORY WOKE WITH A POUNDING head, confused and unaware of her surroundings for a long second. As she blinked her eyes and became more coherent, she recognized the hard plane of Zandar's belly beneath her cheek, and his fingers were stroking her hair in a soothing fashion. Groggily, she blinked harder, as though that would clear her mind, and shifted slightly.

"Are you awake, *lyndrahna*?"

She gave a muffled whimper as agony split her skull when she sat up slowly. "I think so, but maybe this is all just a nightmare." She grasped her head in her hands, groaning again. "Who ran over my skull with a semi?"

Zandar frowned, looking slightly confused. "They did not run over us, Princess Jory. They used some sort of concussive weapon that knocked us both out. We regained consciousness a short time ago, or rather I did, and I assumed you would wake soon after."

She leaned against him, drawing strength and some measure of pain relief just from having his arm around her waist as he cuddled her close. "What do we know about them?"

Zandar shrugged the shoulder she wasn't leaning against. "I've seen very little of our *hosts*." He said the last word with a hint of mocking. "They look like some sort of reptilian race. There's a flurry of activity going on beyond the range of my translator, and our view does not allow me to collect much information."

"Where are we?" She shivered slightly as she realized the ambient temperature around was cool, though it was also kind of dark. Since they had last been in the blinding sun and heat of the desert, it was a strange juxtaposition. "It's like some kind of cave or something, isn't it?"

Zandar looked at his wristband, surprisingly still on his wrist. She assumed if the aliens had wanted to strip their possessions and leave them for dead, they wouldn't have bothered to bring them back to their...wherever this was.

"We seem to be on the peripheral of the underground lake I told you about. Judging from the moisture in the air, and the coolness, I think it's safe to conclude it is most certainly a lake, though one of the largest I've ever seen. It appears to encompass roughly half of the center of the planet, though I can't be entirely sure with radiation having scrambled my wristband to a certain extent."

"How do you know it did?"

Zandar cupped her hip and pulled her closer. "The translator is spotty. That happens sometimes with a language that's new to the translation program, but this is filled with hisses and static, and it's difficult to discern what they're saying when they come near. Not that any have been that close, but I made out a little bit before you woke up when a group passed near us."

She touched his wristband. "Is that how you can speak my language? Or how I understand you?"

Zandar nodded. "As long as you're within range of the device, or I'm within range, it will provide translation for us. You're fuzzy upon occasion now, due to the damage from the radiation, but I still understand you well. I had picked up quite a bit of your language over the past few days, so even if the translator fails completely, we can still communicate."

Impressed, she took his hand. "You've learned English in just a few days?"

"Enough to get by, and if we can't communicate with words, there is always physical communication." His hand slid lower to cup her buttocks, and he squeezed lightly before returning his palm to a more proper position on her waist.

"What are they going to do to us, Zandar?" She tried to hide her fear, but wasn't entirely successful as it leeched through her tone.

"I don't know. If they just wanted our things, they would've left us to die in the desert."

She nodded, pleased his thoughts were similar to her own, indicating she wasn't completely pathetic at this alien survival stuff. "So they might have benign intentions?"

He nodded, his silvery hair cascading down one shoulder as he did so. "It's possible. After all, we aren't confined with manacles or behind any bars, though I'm not convinced there isn't some kind of energy field holding us in. My wristband isn't a reliable source of information at the moment due to the radiation damage, and I'm not going to be testing the theory unless we have no choice."

"So, what? Are we just going to stay here in the cave and wait to see what they want from us?"

He hesitated before answering. "I suppose that's the best thing to do for the moment. I don't believe it will take long for them to come to us. As I said, shortly before you woke there was a group nearby, and they appeared to be checking on us. You were still out, and I feigned sleep, so they moved on. As they talked, they mentioned something about a great feast."

Her heart stuttered with meager hope. "Maybe they're going to throw a huge feast in our honor? They probably haven't seen very many magenta-skinned aliens with tails and silver hair before."

"Or pale-skinned alien women with generous curves, large breasts, and a tight pussy. Not that I intend to share the last bit of information or allow any to discover it for themselves." Zandar winked at her. A second later, his expression grew more serious. "I'm sure we're going to be the center of attention at the dinner, but I haven't determined yet if it's a feast in our honor, or if we're the main course."

Hope fled as she grasped his implications. She might be a dinner buffet for a group of aliens yet. That was an even worse fate than being married off to a prince she didn't know under the guise of being Chiondri. Her stomach rocked and rolled as she waited for the arrival of the people who either had rescued her and Zandar or kidnapped them. Whichever way, they were staying for dinner, but she hoped she wasn't going to be roasting on a spit.

THE ALIENS MUST HAVE realized they were awake, because it was less than ten minutes later before a giggling group of women approached. At least Jory thought they were giggling, judging from the happy cadence of the tone, accompanied by the shy glances they cast toward Zandar before whispering to each other.

"He is certainly a large one," said one of the women. It was strange, because Jory heard a clicking sound coming from the woman, but there was a millisecond delay as Zandar's wristband translated the words in her head. So she was hearing a bit of an echo in her own language, following their primary communication.

"I wonder if he is large between the legs," said another one of the women.

Jory had to struggle not to laugh, and then she realized they might not be women. Just because they were tall, with long hair and pendulous breasts, didn't mean they were the female gender. For these aliens, they might have a completely different classification for gender than male or female anyway. Perhaps they reproduced asexually, or via some other means she couldn't even grasp. Still, it didn't seem like it when they were just speculating on the size of Zandar's member.

The women drew to a stop just a few feet from them. One scurried forward a couple of steps, inclining her head and making more of that tittering giggle sound. She bowed to both of them, and her lime-green hair touched the dirt on the floor as she did so.

Up close, Jory was trying hard not to stare at the alien. She didn't want to be rude, but she'd never seen anything like her. The woman had scales somewhat reminiscent of a reptile, though the arrangement and overlap reminded her more of an armadillo than a lizard. She had a long, thin tail complete with segmented scales, and all the scales on her body glowed luminescent gold with faint undertones of blue-green. She had sideways-slit eyes, and appeared to have an asymmetrical forked tongue when she said to them, "Welcome, guests."

There was a hissing static sound, and though the woman continued to speak, Jory didn't understand much of anything she said. She got a couple of words, including "dinner" and "bath". When the women gestured her forward, she gave Zandar a helpless look as they urged her to her feet. He seemed hesitant, but didn't advise not to go with them. "Are they taking me for a bath?"

He shrugged slightly, even as he nodded. "I believe so, Jory."

She frowned with annoyance, because though she welcomed the idea of getting clean, it meant separation from Zandar and his translation device that allowed her to understand even a little bit of the alien language. "Is it safe?"

He hesitated another second. "I hope so, Jory. If not, I'll find you."

She nodded, putting on a brave face to hide her doubt that he would be able to find her in this underground cavern, if that's what it was, especially if the aliens were intent on eating them. Reluctantly, she followed behind the group of women, who formed a half-circle around her, talking at her in their hissing, clicking sounds she had no way to understand.

They appeared friendly, but she couldn't be certain they weren't leading her to a marinade rather than a bath as they took her from Zandar into a network of passageways and caves. "This is a lovely home you have." It was a stupid thing to say, but she felt rude just maintaining silence as they talked at her.

The women gave her puzzled smiles—at least that's what she thought they were—and she realized they couldn't understand her any better than she could them. With a resigned sigh, she pasted on a smile and went with them to a large puddle of softly bubbling goo.

As she watched, each of the women disrobed, removing the sheer garments that had barely covered their bodies. She stood awkwardly until two of the women indicated she should undress. Jory bit her lip as she slid off the skirt, standing awkwardly in her camisole. Right then, she missed her panties more than she ever could have imagined doing so.

Apparently, the women realized she was uncertain, because they walked into the blue-green water and waved her in. Was it water? She couldn't be certain, because it was thicker than water, but had the undulating wave motion of a babbling brook. Finally, with a deep breath for courage, she peeled off her camisole, laid it beside the skirt, and slipped into the bathing pool.

It was strange, almost like walking into Jell-O, and the substance adhered to her body, while still somehow lapping around her. The women had leaned back and looked relaxed, and she attempted to do the same. At least she was hopeful they weren't trying to marinade her for dinner, since they were joining her in the tub.

Unless they were a group of cannibals. That thought made her stomach churn, but she couldn't imagine the women would be so calm and relaxed about being dinner for their tribe...group...or whatever they called themselves.

The gooey blue-green substance was surprisingly relaxing, forming to her body like the best memory foam mattress ever, and she swore she could practically feel the toxins and dirt leaching from her. Her skin felt smooth when she ran her hand down her body, and she was amazed to realize it had not only cleaned her skin, but had dissolved her body hair.

That outcome mildly alarmed her, but she assumed if it were going to melt her skin as well that she would have felt pain by now. Instead, it was like the ultimate spa treatment—a body scrub, detox, and wax all in one without the pain. A girl could get used to this.

After what seemed like hours, though was probably less than forty-five minutes, the women stirred and waved at her, gesturing it was time to leave the pool. With a sigh of reluctance, she stood up and walked from the goo. It slid off her easily, and when she stood on the rocky bank bordering the substance, she looked down and saw no trace of the goo remaining on her body.

However, her skin was shining and gleaming in a way she had never seen before. All blemishes had disappeared, including the scar from an appendectomy when she was thirteen. Her body was smooth and hairless, and she was glad she had not let her hair into the pool. When one of the women showed her a flat sheet that looked somewhat like a mirror, revealing her reflection, Jory was pleased by what she saw.

There was a faint shimmer to her skin, a golden dusting almost, as if she'd had some kind of sumptuous body lotion with glitter rubbed all over. She looked like she could be a beauty contestant, and when one of the women brought her garments that draped over her shoulder to flow down her body, without actually covering much of her personal assets, she was surprisingly okay with it. It seemed natural to show her body when it was in such a beautiful state, and she couldn't wait to see if Zandar had experienced something similar.

Relaxed and refreshed from the bath, Jory followed behind the women as they led her through more of the caves until they emerged into a large open area. She examined the antechamber closely, surprised to see what looked like bioluminescent lights strung along the walls of the cave, and slabs cut into table-like shapes where hundreds of the aliens had gathered.

Each seat was taken, and there were myriad aliens mingling. She saw smaller ones and taller ones, and she was certain the group she was with were women when she saw the other alien counterpart. The ones she identified as male were taller and leaner, though still muscular, but the thing that set them apart from their females was the huge appendage between their legs that wrapped around their waists a couple of times. A couple of the men seemed to have flung their penises, if that's what they were, over their shoulders, and they flopped down the back, almost touching their buttocks.

Jory's thighs clenched automatically, and she mentally rejected the thought of trying to accept one of those monster genitalia. Not that the aliens were monsters, but those things were huge. It was nothing like the pleasant surprise of finding Zandar was so much larger than the typical earth male. It was just outright fear that made her lower muscles tighten to contemplate mating with one of these aliens. Fortunately, that wasn't her fate. Right?

Shortly after sitting down with the group of females that had taken her to bathe, another woman brought her a clear glass filled with sparkling green liquid. She glanced around, noticing others drinking it, except for the children, and concluded it was some sort of alcoholic beverage. Cautiously, she sniffed the liquid before taking a tiny sip. "Yum." She couldn't help taking another, larger drink of the delicious beverage. It was sweet and bubbly, with undertones of plum, but was like nothing she had ever tasted before. It was actually quite addicting, and she drank an entire glass before she'd realized it.

The women sitting at the table were imbibing just as freely, and she didn't decline when they offered her a refill. This time, Jory forced herself to drink it more slowly, needing to maintain a clear head as she looked for Zandar.

Platters of what she presumed was food began making their way down the tables, and she was relieved to see most of the offerings looked like some sort of plant, so it was quite unlikely either she or Zandar were on tonight's menu.

At that moment, Zandar entered the antechamber from a different cave than she had used. It was clear he had been through a similar bathing ritual, and his skin gleamed with perfection. She couldn't help a little giggle when she noticed his hair was quite a bit shorter than it had been. No longer falling down the middle of his back, it rested at his shoulders. Apparently, he had fallen victim to the depilatory effects of the goo before realizing exactly what it did.

He found her with an unerring accuracy, as though they were already tuned to each other's karmic frequencies. It was a fanciful thought, and she giggled again. When he sat near her, ignoring some of the looks from the women nearby as they pointed to their table and then the set across the room, clearly trying to indicate the men didn't mingle with the women.

She glanced around, belatedly realizing the aliens with the long appendages sat on one side of the large dining area, and the women sat on the other. Only the children moved freely between the groups, but she wasn't about to ask Zandar to leave her side. She leaned against him, inhaling. "You smell divine." He did. He smelled like Zandar, but with some sort of floral scent that was driving her absolutely mad. She wondered if she smelled similarly to him, since she had bathed as well.

"You look gorgeous." He almost growled the words as his gaze settled on her breasts barely covered by the translucent garment. "I'm not sure I like the idea of everyone seeing your body, Jory."

She giggled. "Don't worry about it. I'm just an oddity to them, same as you are. We're the freaks here, Zandar." For some reason, that made her giggle even harder, and she reached for the wine to moisten her dry throat. Before she knew it, she had drunk all that glass too and was reaching for the pitcher to pour a third one when Zandar intercepted her hand. "What?"

"Never drink that with which you aren't familiar, Jory." He looked down at the platter of food nearing them, his brow furrowing. "That also applies to food."

She sighed heavily. "Don't be like that. I'm starving, and this wine is delicious. You really should try some." She giggled again and suddenly realized just how much she had been giggling the last few minutes. Jory giggled upon occasion, but it wasn't something she did often. She wasn't a teenager and hadn't been for a long time.

For some reason, everything was funny, and she eyed the wine doubtfully. It must have a higher alcohol content than she was accustomed to back on Earth. Deciding reluctantly to take his advice and forgo more wine, she took her hand from the empty cup, but accepted the tray he handed her with a defiant look.

After examining it closely, she took a serving of something long and silvery-blue that resembled seaweed. It was wrapped around something gray-brown, and while it wasn't the most appetizing thing she'd ever seen, she was hungry enough to try it. She passed the tray to the woman sitting beside her before casting a discreet glance at the table around her. There were no signs of silverware anywhere, and everyone was using their hands. *When in Rome*, she decided with a shrug.

Carefully, she picked at the silvery-blue outer wrapping, pulling off a section, along with some of the substance inside it. Zandar gave her a fierce frown when she brought it to her nose. Resisting the urge to stick out her tongue (and giggle), she sniffed lightly. It smelled a bit like tulips and roasted pig. Intrigued, and a little alarmed at the idea of such a combination, she hesitantly put it in her mouth.

Jory couldn't hold back a moan of appreciation as the food melted on her tongue. A flavor explosion hit her taste buds, and she moaned again. It was like an orgasm in her mouth, and she couldn't identify its exact flavor profile, but it was the most amazing thing ever. As she reached for more, she told Zandar, "I may never leave here."

His expression remained solemn, bordering on stern. "You will leave here, Jory, because a Gentarren ship will be coming to pick us up any time now."

"Why are you such a party pooper?" She stuck her tongue out at him, and then giggled again. To lessen the sting, in case he didn't realize she was teasing, she leaned against him to bump his shoulder in a gentle way. At the first touch of his skin against hers, heat flared in Jory, and she was abruptly aroused. As she contemplated pulling the big alien onto the table and having her way with him, Jory saw the people were spreading out from the tables, and the genders were mixing.

Her eyes widened when she realized just how much they were mixing as the women danced sensuously around their partners, and more than one female had her mate's freakishly large genitalia wrapped around her, as though anchoring her against her male counterpart. Compelled by morbid curiosity, she peered closer and saw the alien penises, if that's what they were, had disappeared between the legs of more than one of the female aliens. "Oh my god, we're in the middle of an orgy."

Zandar smirked at her. "Did I not tell you to avoid the food and drink? It appears either the food or the wine has lowered everyone's inhibitions. I assume the wine, because the children scurried away, but they ate first."

She rolled her eyes. "You have to take such pleasure in being right all the time. You can be such a downer sometimes, Zandar."

Without even realizing it, Jory's hand had crept between her thighs, and she was stroking her own clit as she spoke to him. With a small cry, she pulled her hand from between her legs and gave him a look of concern. "Get me out of here before I do something crazy. Please." He sighed, appearing annoyed, but his eyes sparkled with amusement. She would have smacked him for being a jackass, but she was afraid to touch him at all lest she jump on him and hump her way to an orgasm.

The sight of aliens undulating around her was arousing in a way she couldn't explain. There was nothing sexy to her about them having sex, except for the expressions on the aliens' faces. It was clear they were into each other, and the world around them had ceased to exist. As Zandar took her hand and led her from the antechamber, she couldn't help wondering if every meal ended like this, or if it was just a special occasion. As they wandered the caves, she paused to lean against the wall as her head spun and her heart raced. "Do you know where we're going?"

"I believe I can get us back to the place where we woke, but I can't be sure how to get us out of this underground city. That depends on how reliable my wristband remains. The exit appears to be approximately forty *konars* from here, but I can't be certain."

She groaned. "Forty *konars* isn't like a hundred million miles, is it? 'Cause there's no way I'm going to make it that far without an orgasm or two." She giggled again.

He crossed his arms over his shoulders as he shook his head. "It's about two kilometers in Earth distance."

Jory's body burned, and she started scratching as though trying to relieve an itch she couldn't reach. She cast a glance at Zandar, deciding he was the sexiest he'd ever been. Was that the wine, the bath that had made him so smooth and polished, or just the fact she was hornier than she'd ever been in her life?

It was natural to draw closer to him and begin tugging at his khaki mesh. "It's too bad you didn't accept one of the alien garments, Zandar." Thankfully, during the days trapped on the shuttle after they had become lovers, she had learned how to take off the body armor, and he was soon stripped below the waist.

Zandar didn't try to stop her, but he definitely wasn't assisting her in her quest. Instead, he planted his feet wide apart, leaned against the wall, and had the gall to look bored. He seemed annoyed by her actions, but his hard cock revealed the truth when it sprang free from his body armor.

With a sigh of pleasure, Jory stroked the head for a second before dropping to her knees. She was going to banish that annoyed look one way or the other. She licked her lips before running her tongue across the head of his large penis, and he uttered a groan in the back of his throat. Pleased to discover he wasn't as unmoved as he appeared, she stretched her mouth as wide as she could to take even a portion of his large cock.

She sucked and licked him until he was hard in her mouth, swelling beyond the confines of her lips. With a sigh of reluctance, she took him from her mouth, but continued to lick the tip and around the shaft until Zandar abruptly lifted her into his arms, spinning her and pinning her to the wall where he had been just a moment before. She expected him to take her then and there, but instead, Zandar lifted her higher, supporting her by the thighs as he crouched down, his mouth moving between her legs.

He had tasted her before, but she was so sensitive and aroused, probably from the alien wine, that he had her coming with a few swipes of his tongue. Zandar didn't ease up, coaxing another orgasm from her before he stood up and moved her into position.

A moment later, his large cock surged inside her, stretching as it always did, but no longer with pain. She had grown accustomed to his size, and she welcomed every inch of him. Jory twisted and bucked against the wall, arching her hips frantically against Zandar as he took her with equal intensity. She knew her increased ardor was marginally attributable to the wine, but there was nothing to explain his except pure desire for her.

She tightened her thighs around his waist as her sheath convulsed, urging Zandar to spill his seed inside her. They moaned together as they came, their bodies shaking under the force of the release.

At some point, Zandar's knees must have given out, because they collapsed to the floor, though they remained joined. She was vaguely aware of the fine dust under her knees and against the tops of her feet, but she was too tired to care.

No, she discovered she wasn't *that* worn out when she shifted slightly, and he hardened again. "I think maybe you were right about the wine," she said with a small giggle as she started riding him once more.

"I'm sure I was, but I can't be sorry you indulged in a glass or two, Jory. If it has this side effect, we'll have to secure a supply to take with us when we leave here."

With another giggle, she surrendered to the passion coursing through her, feeling like she could never get enough of Zandar.

Chapter Eight

APPARENTLY, THE ALIEN wine came with a hell of a hangover. Her head ached almost as badly when she woke as it had the first time the day before, and that had been due to the concussive weapon the aliens had used. Zandar was shaking her arm, and she batted at him, wanting to sleep longer.

"Jory, you must wake now."

She opened her eyes slowly, looking up at him from her spot on the dirt. "Why? Tired. My head hurts." God, she sounded so whiny.

His lips twitched, and apparently, he agreed she was a whining brat. "I've received a signal from a Gentarren ship. They're going to land on the surface in roughly thirty minutes, and we need to meet them outside of the caverns. The ship is too large to navigate through the network of caves."

"Can't they just beam us up or something?"

He frowned. "What is this beam up?"

With an irritated sigh, she sat up, and her head spun dizzily. "Never mind. I guess you guys don't have teleporters or something?"

He arched a brow. "You mean a matter re-arranger and transporter?"

She shrugged. "I guess. Do I look like sci-fi girl to you?"

Sanders shook his head. "You look like an inebriated wanton." His lips twitched, and he grinned at her. "I find it charming, Jory, but you must get up now so we can meet the ship." As he spoke, Zandar bent down and lifted her to her feet, ensuring she was steady as they started walking. "To answer your question, no, we don't have matter re-arrangers or transporters. That's still theoretical science. I'm surprised Earthlings have gotten that far."

She rolled her eyes at the dig toward the barbaric Earthlings, reluctantly admitting, "It's just in a TV show. Or some movies. I don't know. Maybe some books too. Science fiction isn't really my genre of choice. I prefer the smutty romances, though there is something to be said for a dashing alien spiriting you away to another world and having his way with you." She smiled slightly, though it hurt her entire face. She truly was a miserable mess as she followed him from the cave, moving gingerly.

The few aliens they passed seemed to be in a similar state, and Jory couldn't imagine they did this every night. It must have been a special occasion, either coinciding with their arrival, or in honor of their stay, but she couldn't imagine an entire society could function if they had orgies every night and massive hangovers every day.

They finally emerged from the system of caves about twenty-five minutes later, and Jory was sad she hadn't been able to tell her new friends goodbye or thank them for the interesting experiences, amazing food, and fabulous orgasms.

Casting a sideways glance at Zandar through her lashes, she supposed that was more do to him than them, though the wine had certainly enhanced her pleasure. She was mildly regretful they hadn't been able to secure a supply of their own to bring with them, but decided it was perhaps for the best. She couldn't function like this all the time either.

A large ship made from the familiar semitransparent material waited for them, and she was relieved, because it was hotter than hell outside. The two suns were directly overhead, beaming down on them, and though wearing only a gossamer alien garment should have embarrassed her, she was relieved not to have to deal with clothes in the ferocious heat. She only hoped he had some spare clothing on board that large ship—or kept the thermostat on high, or she'd go from boiling to freezing in no time.

As they neared, a door opened, gliding out and downward to form a ramp that Zandar led her up. The cool metal of the ship felt good against her hot feet, singed from the sand just by the short walk from the caves to the ship. She wanted to stay there all day and soak in the soothing coolness, but that wasn't an option due to someone waiting for them.

He was a large alien, though not quite as large as Zandar, with purple skin and gold eyes. A thick thatch of black hair across the top of his head was the only body hair in sight, though he might have more underneath a khaki suit nearly identical to Zandar's.

Zandar arched a brow. "I didn't expect to see you on this voyage, Kendrick."

"Kendrick? As in Prince Kendrick?" asked Jory, her mouth hanging open. Good Lord, here she was in front of royalty, albeit alien royalty, wearing nothing more than a wisp of fabric to hide her generous curves. With a small squeal, she ducked behind Zandar in a belated attempt to preserve her modesty. "I need some clothes," she hissed to her lover.

Kendrick frowned. "You have allowed the princess to walk around naked?"

Forgetting her embarrassment, Jory stepped out from behind Zandar again, hands on her hips. "I'm not Chiara. Er, Chiondri. I'm her roommate, and I think that little...well, I won't say the word in front of a prince, but she set me up to take her place. She put a biochip in me, which now says I'm her when I'm not her."

Kendrick looked confused, and he wore a massive scowl. "You claim you aren't the princess?"

She heaved a sigh. "She's your fiancée, so shouldn't you know what she looks like?"

He shrugged. "Chiondri has had months to alter her appearance, and I didn't spend that much time with her, so I can't be sure. However, she seemed more biddable than you."

Jory wanted to stick out her tongue at the prince, but figured that might be some kind of breach of protocol that would lead to execution. Instead, she settled for saying in an overly sweet tone, "Apparently she wasn't that biddable, Your Highness, or she wouldn't have run out on you."

To her surprise, Kendrick and Zandar both laughed heartily. "You are a delight, Princess Jory," said Kendrick.

Jory frowned, now the one confused. "Jory? Princess?"

Kendrick put a hand on her arm to draw her forward to walk beside him, ignoring Zandar's low growl of disapproval. "While you...slept, Zandar had time to explain the situation to me, Jory, and he believes you aren't Chiondri. I was just teasing. I wish to gain your help in reacquiring the princess, so I hope I did not provoke offense."

Her mouth dropped open, and she stared at Kendrick for a moment as Zandar came to stand beside her, his arm going around her waist to pull her against him in a barbaric display of territorialism that she couldn't help appreciating slightly. He was clearly staking his claim. "Is this some sort of alien prank then?" She tipped her head back to look up at her alien lover. "Zandar, you actually have a sense of humor? I'm shocked."

Kendrick roared with laughter again, though Zandar maintained a straight expression "She certainly has you figured out, doesn't she, brother?"

Jory took two more steps before his words penetrated her brain, and she stopped suddenly, whirling to face Zandar. "Brother? Is that the same as it is on Earth, like a friend calling you bro or buddy?"

Zandar hesitated for a second before shaking his head. "No, it's not like an Earth custom. Kendrick is my half-brother."

She couldn't help shaking her head as her brain processed what she had just learned. "You're a prince?"

Kendrick had been eyeing them with interest, and now smiled. "You didn't tell her you were a prince of Gentarres?"

Zandar frowned at him. "I am many things, and a prince of Gentarres is low on the list. I am from Karadis first."

Kendrick rolled his eyes, clearly rehashing an old argument. "Yes, yes I know our father is a despicable despoiler of virgins, and your mother is a saint. Your people are the only ones with any moral compass, et cetera." He turned from his brother to smile at her. "Jory, Zandar is a prince, though he refuses to acknowledge the title, and he certainly won't inherit anything tangible."

She glared at him. "It's because he's illegitimate, isn't it? That's a pretty crappy way to treat your family—"

He held up a hand, his lips twitching in a familiar way, and as she stared at his face, she recognized certain similarities between himself and Zandar. "No, it's because I'm older, and we have three other brothers all in line before Zandar. Should he wish to take up some sort of role, such as ambassador or attaché to the Royal Family, Father would welcome him into the fold. Instead, Zandar chooses to maintain distance because our father slighted his mother."

"It's not that simple or as childish as you make it sound," said Zandar, his mouth tight. He looked at Jory. "He wasn't free to marry her after leading her to believe he was. He didn't tell her he already had two other wives, and she refused to be his third when she discovered she carried me."

Kendrick gesticulated wildly with one finger. "Yes, brother, but he did propose. Your side always forgets that."

Jory's head spun, and nausea crept up her throat. It had nothing to do with their conversation, which she thought she was following fairly well. It was simply illness that overwhelmed her. "Zandar, I don't feel well. I think the wine..."

As fast as she could manage it, Jory turned from both the men before vomiting on the metal floor of the corridor. She was vaguely aware of collapsing against Zandar, and of his arms enfolding her as he lifted and carried her down the hallway that looked so much like the ship they had been on before. She was certain he took her to the medical bay, though that was the last thing she saw as her eyes closed.

Chapter Nine

JORY'S HEAD STILL SPUN when she woke a few minutes later. A groan escaped her as she sat up, and a large hand on her arm slowed her progress.

"Easy there. Your head is probably still spinning."

She nodded, instantly regretting the motion as she cupped her forehead and peered at the alien speaking to her. This one appeared to be female, since she had more of the thick black hair, a smaller build, leaner waist, and visible breasts. Nothing like the generous girls Jory hauled around, but certainly more than Kendrick or Zandar. "What happened?"

"Here, take this." The woman held out a cylinder, seeming surprised when Jory put her mouth around it. "You're familiar with our medicine?"

She nodded as the mist seeped into her mouth and dispersed throughout her body. Within seconds, the nausea had eased, and her throbbing headache faded. "That stuff's amazing."

The woman smiled. "Yes, it is. I'm Healer Kythar, and you are Princess Jory."

Jory's face flushed. "I'm not really a princess. I wish Zandar would stop saying that."

Kythar smiled. "It is good to be a man's princess, isn't it?" A hint of sadness crept across her features, but was gone when she blinked. "Now, can you tell me about your recent events, so we can narrow down the problem?"

Jory nodded, launching into a clumsy explanation of being kidnapped, marooned on a desert planet, and rescued by aliens in time for their orgy ritual.

As she spoke, Kythar nodded, her expression neutral. "Have you had sexual relations with anyone recently?"

Feeling inexplicably shy about the admission, she nodded and mumbled Zandar's name.

The doctor nodded again before turning to her computer. She spoke to it in her language. Jory didn't know if that would be Gentarren, Karadisian, or something else. A few moments later, the computer began flashing through images so quickly her eyes couldn't follow. "What's it doing?"

"The computer is attempting to identify the alien species from Planet G-17B."

Jory tried to follow the images, getting glimpses here and there of alien species, but not enough detail to have a good mental picture of them. "They all appear humanoid. That's not what I expected from aliens."

Kythar nodded. "We don't have a firm explanation, but we have two viable theories. The first is simply like attracts like, so we're more inclined to find aliens that look similar to us. Who knows how many other alien species we have overlooked because we didn't recognize they were alive or sentient?"

That made sense, but she still asked, "And the second theory?"

"It's more mythical than reality, of course, but some people like to believe there was an original species from which we all descended, one that mastered space travel, genetic manipulation, terraforming...oh, myriad skills one would need to colonize an entire galaxy." The healer's skeptical tone left little doubt she didn't believe that theory.

"It's a nice thought, but the other idea makes more sense." Jory shifted as her nausea peaked again before settling. "What's wrong with me, Doctor Kythar?"

The purple woman frowned. "Doctor?"

"I mean Healer."

Kythar nodded. "Healer is the closest word the translator could discern to describe my position, I suppose. A doctor must be like a healer?"

"Um, sometimes," said Jory with a small smile, though not wishing to delve deeply into the problems plaguing the medical system. "Do you have a diagnosis for me, Healer Kythar?"

"First, is this the alien group that rescued you?" She moved aside so Jory could see the display more clearly.

It was definitely the same group of aliens, unless they had doppelgangers somewhere in the galaxy. "Yes, that looks like them."

"Ah, these are the Bhaziers, or at least that's how we know them. We've had limited contact with them, and their language is difficult for our translators to understand."

"Maybe it wasn't all radiation damage," said Jory before explaining their communications difficulties with the Bhaziers.

"You said they fed you a feast and offered a green beverage?" At Jory's nod, Kythar said something to the computer again. She cleared her throat before turning back to face her. "Did the evening culminate in certain amorous activities?"

Jory's eyes widened. "It was a freaking orgy, if that's what you mean."

Kythar blinked her golden eyes. "Yes, that's exactly what I meant. I hesitate to be indelicate, but did you partake in the orgy, Jory?"

Her eyes widened, and she shook her head before pausing. "Well, I did, but not with the aliens. Just with Zandar..." She trailed off with a groan. "Have I picked up some kind of alien sex virus?"

Kythar shook her head. "No. The ritual in which you partook last night was the Mating Frenzy. As far as we can glean, Bhaziers females only come into heat once per year naturally. However, a type of algae that grows in the caves of their underground city produces an intense estrus that leads to arousal and ovulation, so they have frequent Frenzies."

Jory's head spun, but she didn't think it was a physical reaction. This was purely a fear-based response as the healer's words penetrated her brain. "Does the algae work on other species?"

Kythar had a glint of sympathy in her eyes. "It appears so, Jory."

She shook her head, rejecting the words even before the healer spoke them.

"You're pregnant."

Chapter Ten

JORY STARED AT THE healer, shaking her head, still refusing to accept the diagnosis. "That makes no sense. Even if I were pregnant, and I couldn't possibly be already, I wouldn't be showing symptoms for weeks. How could you see if I was pregnant if I conceived last night?"

Kythar spoke to her computer in her language, and a three-dimensional diagram appeared before Jory, instantly recognizable as the human form. Under Kythar's direction, the computer zoomed in on the pelvic region, filling a space at least three feet by three feet on the display. Jory couldn't deny the baby-looking thing inside her was probably real. "Are you sure it isn't some sort of alien parasite?" she asked almost hopefully, wondering if it would really be any worse to be in an "Alien" movie scenario than to be pregnant with an alien baby by a man she barely knew?

The healer shook her head, looking regretful, though perhaps her lips twitched just a bit with amusement. "No, that is certainly a fetus. If you look closely, you'll see the typical humanoid features, and there's the tail of a Karadis baby, arm and leg buds, and an oversized head."

Her head whirled, and she didn't know which thing to focus on first. Finally Jory asked, "It has an oversized head? Is it going to stay out of proportion?"

Kythar shook her head. "That's doubtful, Jory. It's a normal stage of development for both Karadisian and Gentarren fetuses, and according to my computer, is also typical for Homo sapiens."

Hysteria swelled inside her, making it difficult to breathe. "You know what's not typical? It's not typical to be able to see you're pregnant the day after you got that way." Jory didn't know exactly who she was angry with, or why she was so angry, but it filled her, making her want to scream.

Kythar consulted her computer again, making several low noises clearly intended more for her own ears than anyone else's. They sounded a bit like "Aha." "Here we are. This is the Intergalactic Interspecies Breeding Database. It gives us the most favorable and least favorable species with which to breed. Of course, a lot of species can't mingle—or at least genetically they can't—but humans and Karadisian clearly can." She gave Jory a small smile with that observation. "According to this, a normal human pregnancy is forty weeks. Does that sound right?"

Jory nodded, her stomach surging with nausea again. "Yeah, and it's like four or six weeks before you find out you're pregnant back on my world."

"A typical Karadis pregnancy is fifteen weeks. We have to figure in that Zandar is also half-Gentarren, and their typical pregnancy is twelve weeks..." She trailed off, clearly mentally calculating, before making another hum that sounded like "Aha." "I see. According to the database, humans and Karadisians have blended a few times, and the genetics are highly compatible. There appears to be a catalyst when the DNA of the two species combine, accelerating the pregnancy."

Jory blinked, unable to get a grasp on what she was hearing. "What does that even mean? How can it be a catalyst?"

"The genes just happen to mesh well, and the dominant traits of each species comes in to play, and when you factor in the Gentarren Growth Factor, it's little wonder the pregnancy progresses so quickly."

Her head ached and nausea was returning quickly, burning a trail up her esophagus. "So how accelerated is accelerated?" If the fetus was already visible, at least with alien technology, how long until she was ready to give birth? The thought made her want to giggle hysterically, but she restrained the urge, because it held more than a hint of panic, and she couldn't surrender to that right now.

"It's a rough estimate, of course, but I think your pregnancy is progressing roughly four times faster than the average Earthling pregnancy. So perhaps in ten weeks?"

Jory shook her head, pointing to the image of the fetus still on the display in front of her. "I don't know much about babies, but that one doesn't look like it's only four days along."

Kythar nodded, looking closer at her computer. "The computer is estimating the gestational age at five weeks. To me, that indicates you conceived before the alien Mating Frenzy in which you partook."

Jory wanted to continue to refuse to believe what she was hearing, but it was starting to make an odd sort of sense. In fact, it had been roughly a week since she and Zandar had become lovers, and that would put her four weeks along. That still meant Kythar's estimate was off, so she was likely to have this baby before ten weeks had passed, but at least she didn't have to worry about popping out a baby ala "Alien" right then.

"I can't believe I didn't even think about birth control." It hadn't even come to mind. Why would it though? From what she knew of science, which was admittedly not as much as she should, it was usually difficult for species to interbreed, even if they were close genetic matches. Not getting pregnant was supposed to be a no-brainer when it came to alien flings.

This was officially the worst week ever.

"So what are my options, Kythar?"

"You can give birth, terminate, or transfer the pregnancy to a willing host. Do you have a willing host?"

Jory tipped her head sideways. "I don't suppose male Karadisians can get pregnant or carry babies, can they?"

Kythar laughed gently. "No, unfortunately not. The same is also true of Gentarren males."

"Do they have surrogates or something that I could hire if I decide to go through with this?" How could she go through with it? The idea of having an alien baby was terrifying. Hell, she would have been freaked out by the idea of carrying a fully human baby right then, with no job or partner. Zandar wasn't her partner. Was he?

"Of course. There are services that provide surrogates to carry pregnancies, but the process does take some time, and with your pregnancy progressing so quickly, you would have about three days to find a replacement womb."

Jory's heart sank with disappointment at the thought, because it sounded impossible to find a surrogate in three days. She knew she could terminate, and that was the sensible choice, especially in light of the fact her child was an alien hybrid, and if he or she was born magenta-skinned, they would never fit in on Earth.

If she had the baby, she would either have to give it to Zandar and leave it behind, or give up her own life on her home planet. Other than her mother, there wasn't a whole lot keeping her on Earth, and that was a startling discovery. Close to twenty-nine, and she still had little to show for it. She had no home of her own, no lover or partner, no children, and not even a career. Heck, she didn't even have a steady job.

That didn't mean she was ready to start a new life on a distant alien planet either. She didn't have a job there, she wouldn't even know how to find a home, and she had no idea if she had a partner, or a lover, or just a temporary fling in Zandar. The only definite thing she had was a child on the way. Her head hurt from trying to make a decision, and she nodded to Kythar's suggestion that she have a nap.

To her surprise, the healer escorted her from the medical bay and down the ship's corridor to a small room clearly meant for guests. It was utilitarian, with a single bunk and some equipment and machinery she didn't recognize. Jory lay down, and though her thoughts should have kept her awake, along with her fears, tiredness overwhelmed her instead, and she fell into a dreamless sleep.

A TAP AT HER DOOR WOKE her, though she didn't know how much time had passed, since she had no timepiece and didn't understand their time system anyway. "Come in," she called hoarsely.

Though it wasn't a complete shock to see Zandar standing in her room a second later, she wasn't exactly ready to deal with him yet either. Jory still hadn't decided how she was going to proceed, or even if she should tell him just yet what the problem was.

It was a lot to thrust upon someone she had known only a week or so—someone who had kidnapped her and stolen her from her life and given her an alien baby. Not that she hadn't participated actively in that part. In fact, she had been an eager participant, and she wasn't trying to deny the conception was equally her responsibility.

"How do you feel?" As he asked, Zandar sat on the edge of the bunk.

Jory scooted up so her back was pressed against the metal wall, taking a moment to evaluate how she felt. "I'm still nauseated, and I wouldn't mind another shot of that medicine Kythar gave me, but I think I'll live."

He flinched. "Was there some doubt about you living? Are you dying, Princess Jory?"

The panic in his tone was gratifying, letting her know he would be at least somewhat devastated if she croaked. Quickly, she reached out to touch his hand with her own. "No, I'm not dying. I'll be fine in a few weeks." Understatement of the year. She'd be anything but fine. She'd no longer be physically ill in a few weeks, but she would be a mother if she decided to proceed.

"What *is* wrong with you? I asked the healer, but of course she refused to tell me since we're not family."

Jory licked her lips, hesitating on how to proceed. Should she just tell him, or should she continue to hide the fact until she had decided whether or not to terminate? Did the decision lie fully with her, or was his input valued as well?

Of course she valued his input, but she didn't know his legal status. If she decided she didn't want to remain pregnant, and he decided she should have the baby, did he have the right to override her decision? Could he keep her from terminating if he chose?

She opened her mouth, planning to give him some sort of vague explanation for her illness, but burst into tears instead. Ugly, rasping sobs ripped from her throat, and tears poured from her eyes. Jory knew she was not her most attractive when she cried. Some women made it look good, but not her.

Still, Zandar didn't flinch or try to get away. Instead, he drew her into his arms to offer comfort. The solid plain of his chest her against her cheek was surprisingly soothing, as were his arms around her. As he held her, she realized she wasn't alone. Perhaps that was a naïve belief, but she didn't really think Zandar would abandon her or the child.

"Will you please tell me what's wrong with you?" His chest rumbled against her ear when he spoke, concern lacing his tone. "I fear the worst. I don't like not knowing what's happening. Was it the wine?"

Just as suddenly as she'd started crying, Jory burst out laughing instead. "I thought it was to start with, but no, it wasn't the wine." She giggled for another moment, until her last giggle turned to hiccups. Only after they had passed was she able to speak again. "Apparently, our species are like fire and gasoline. We're super combustible, or super compatible. I'm not sure what you'd consider it, except a bit of a disaster."

Zandar frowned, his confusion evident. "Please explain, Jory. I know what gasoline is, and of course I realize what fire is, but what does that have to do with your state of health? Were you burned somewhere?" He inspected her from the top of her head down to her knees, clearly looking at all of her visible skin to find where she had been scorched.

She laughed again, though reined it in sharply when it threatened to turn to a gale of hysteria instead of amusement. "I'm not on fire, and I haven't been burned. I'm pregnant, Zandar."

With a fierce frown, he crossed his arms over his chest. "Why did you not tell me you were involved with a man on Earth?" His scowl deepened, and his shoulders straightened. "It doesn't matter. You're mine now, and I will not return you to him."

Jory considered being offended by his barbaric pronouncement, but rather than alarm her, it soothed her fears, though she wasn't ready to let him be the dominant caveman he clearly craved to be. "I'm not in a relationship back on Earth, but if I wanted to go back home, you wouldn't keep me here."

His eyes widened, and he clearly grasped the implications immediately. "I will keep you as long as I wish while my child is inside you, Jory."

How could she swing from happy to exasperated so quickly? Oh, that was an easy answer. Zandar was an infuriating, much-too-sexy man, and he upset her equilibrium on an alarmingly wild basis.

"Just so we're clear, Zandar, you don't own me, and I've put up with way more of your nonsense than I should have. You've dragged me around, stranded me on a desert planet, exposed me to aliens and their orgies, and you've knocked me up. If I want to go home, I expect you to take me home right now."

He flinched, either from her shrill tone or her words. After a moment, he nodded. "I apologize. I have been too dictatorial. Of course if you wish to return to your Earth, I will take you, but I will not leave you there. I'll be by your side the entire time." His eyes narrowed, the vibrant purple holding an unmistakable glint of determination. "If you insist on settling on that backwater planet, I'll find a way to blend in, but I won't leave my child behind."

She was touched by his words, even as they slightly annoyed her. As usual, he wasn't listening to her, but she decided that was perhaps unfair too. Eventually, Zandar had listened to her and had believed she wasn't Chiondri. He had vouched for her with his brother, and he had tried to save her life more than once.

It was clear he cared about her, or at least the life they had created together, and that was worth dealing with the macho bullshit. She could have had the equivalent of an intergalactic deadbeat dad, so this had to be better than that.

"I don't necessarily want to go back to Earth, at least right away, Zandar. To be honest, I'm not sure what to do. The healer mentioned surrogates, or I could terminate, but I'm going to have it." It wasn't until she spoke the words that she realized she had already made up her mind long ago. "I'm going to have our baby." She felt the need to modify her statement to change "it" to baby.

He looked pleased, with a touch of smugness. Or maybe it was pure male ego from his own virility. "You'll come stay with me on Karadis." When she exhaled sharply, his expression softened. "I mean would you like to come stay with me on Karadis, Jory?"

She found herself nodding, though she wasn't sure that was really the best choice. Really, where else should she go at this point? At least on his planet, a magenta-skinned baby wouldn't be that strange, and she wouldn't have to fear government officials or people with bad intentions trying to steal her child and subject it to horrible tests.

Maybe that was a fanciful fear engendered by years of popular media, but she couldn't shake the terror once the idea had taken hold. "Thank you, Zandar. I would enjoy that very much." She sounded so stiff and formal, much more so than she wanted to, but she was lost on how to proceed as well. What was she going to do on his planet? At least Zandar would be there to help her and guide her.

He nodded, looking satisfied. "Excellent. I'll tell Kendrick he's on his own for his bride hunt and have him drop us at the nearest inhabited planet to get home to Karadis. I'll let my mother know we're coming. She'll be quite pleased to meet you."

Jory managed a small smile, hoping he was being honest or not naïve. Would his mother be happy to welcome a human into her life, and as the mother of her grandchild? She didn't know, and she had no reason to fear the other woman's reception, but she had never seemed to make a good impression on her previous boyfriends' mothers.

She wasn't sure why that was, and had often attributed it to the women themselves. She had discovered a pattern over the years, and that was she tended to draw mama's boys for some reason. When she didn't automatically defer to their mothers too, it had created conflict between her and her previous boyfriends, and the mothers had always won.

Jory had been fine with that, because who wanted someone who always wanted to please their mommy? Still, the idea of Zandar turning out to be a mama's boy was unsettling, and she only hoped his mother liked her.

Chapter Eleven

KARADIS WAS A SHINING jewel, with pristine lakes, a large ocean surrounding the single continent, one sun, and seven moons of varying sizes, with at least five visible in the sky at any given time. Because of the moons, the tides were frequent and fierce, but that was the only mar on the beautiful haven that Jory could determine.

Most of the people lived inland to avoid random tides and tsunamis that might hit unexpectedly, and Zandar's home was perched at the top of the highest mountain. Of course it did, because he had failed to mention that not only was he a Gentarren prince, but he was also a prince of Karadis and heir to the throne as the next High Prince, since he had no sisters.

His mother was the Royal Queen, and his uncle Hyzaar was the current High Prince. Their society was a matriarchy, and the genders blended harmoniously—which was interesting, because all the men were just as dominating and powerfully built as Zandar. Well, perhaps not quite as large as him, with a few exceptions. His uncle was a broad-shouldered, massive man who appeared to be the standard of Karadisian male beauty, judging by the sheer number of women who hung on his every word and likely graced his bed.

It was clear Zandar's magenta coloring came from the Gentarren genes, because most of the Karadis population were a shimmery gold color, with platinum blonde hair and ice-blue or pale-green eyes. She had worried about their baby not fitting in, but Zandar didn't seem to have any issue blending in to the society with his unusual coloring.

Jory was intimidated her first few days on the planet, feeling rather like a curvy gal plucked down in the middle of Fashion Week in New York and expected to strut the runway in a size negative-two evening gown. Fortunately, the people were as beautiful on the inside as the outside, and she soon felt at home.

Izaria, Zandar's mother, had been a welcome surprise. She was gracious and charming, and she didn't seem to care that Jory was human. As they enjoyed an afternoon tea a week after her arrival, Zandar having been banished from the event by his mother with a gentle, but insistent, dismissal, the older woman said, "I'm pleased to see my son in love. I don't care about your species. I just hope this will help him choose to settle down here on the home planet instead of pursuing bounty missions with his uncles."

Jory didn't disputes Izaria's assumption that Zandar loved her. It was too personal a topic to dissect over tea. Plus she kind of liked entertaining the idea her alien lover felt more for her than just passion and concern for his child in her stomach.

He had instilled her in his suite from the moment they had arrived at his palace, and he had been by her side for most of each day since. Nights were spent in blissful exploration, and she had discovered she was quite insatiable in the bedroom, at least with Zandar.

"I hope you're right, Izaria." It felt strange to call the queen by her given name, but the other woman had insisted from the start. "I already feel lost here, without a job or purpose other than growing Zandar's baby. I wouldn't like to think of him being gone for long stretches of time, especially when the baby is still an infant." At least the acceleration ended with pregnancy, and she had been relieved to learn humans, Gentarrens, and Karadisians all had a similar time of development from infancy to adulthood.

There had been no hope of hiding her pregnancy, even had she chosen to do so. Zandar had announced it with pride from practically the moment he had introduced her to his mother and uncle, but it hadn't taken her long to start showing.

She was only two weeks along, which put her somewhere between eight and ten weeks for a normal Earth pregnancy, but she already had a visible baby bump, and her breasts had grown larger. Jory was kind of concerned about the fast changes, but was trying to embrace what Kythar had told her about an accelerated rate of growth, confirmed by the palace healer.

"Zandar will be here for you and the baby. As will I, Princess Jory."

Jory's cheeks flushed at the affectionate nickname that somehow had spread among Zandar's family. Perhaps they had heard him call her that once or twice, or maybe they had hoped she would soon officially bear the title of Princess.

Jory had found herself considering the idea, though it was insane after just a week in this life. Still, she couldn't deny she had never felt more at home, and her alien lover had a way of making her feel loved, protected, and secure. She was still nervous about giving birth and raising an alien child, but Jory could see herself building a life here on Karadis, if she could figure out her purpose in this alien culture.

There was still so much to learn, though Izaria had generously provided her with a cultural tutor, with whom she met a few times per week, so she was optimistic she would find a way to fit in. The main question remaining was whether she would fit in as some sort of royal consort, just the mother of the possible heir of the Karadisian throne—assured if she carried a girl, and possible if it was a boy, though any sisters born after him would supersede his claim—or as Zandar's partner and wife.

He hadn't mentioned anything about marriage or bonding, as they called it on Karadis. Jory didn't know if he was giving her time to adjust, if he was determining how he felt as well, or if he had no intention of ever asking her to bond.

She knew she was rushing things by hoping for some kind of proposal, and common sense would dictate a refusal even if he did ask her to be his bride in the near future. That didn't mean she couldn't indulge in some fantasies, and she had even asked her cultural advisor about wedding customs on their planet.

After tea with the queen, Jory returned to the suite to find Zandar pacing, though he seemed to still as soon as she arrived. Did she have that effect on him? He certainly had a soothing effect on her. Any time she was feeling anxious, he seemed to realize and would be by her side with an arm around her waist, or a supportive hand on her hip. Surprisingly, he was a touchy-feely kind of guy, but she enjoyed the attention. Her body tingled, and she realize she wouldn't mind some attention right then.

He smiled at her. "Did you enjoy your time with my mother?"

Jory nodded. "Izaria is a lovely woman." She truly was, and it was a nice change to get along with her boyfriend's mother. If one could call Zandar a boyfriend. Still, she had been shocked by how welcoming the ruling leader of a whole planet could be to an Earthling whom she had never met before.

"I think your mother's a bit of a softy. She's hoping my presence, or at least the baby, will keep you here at home, so you can assume your royal duties rather than pursuing the trade of your people."

The Karadis race were good hunters, and that had naturally evolved into becoming trackers over the centuries. Their planet produced some of the best bounty hunters in the galaxy, and their services were highly sought after. Jory liked to tease him upon occasion that clearly there was a problem with their system, since he had scooped her up instead of Chiondri, and he always growled a gruff reply that things had worked out exactly as intended.

His eyes widened as she began to unfasten the loops holding the pretty golden garment on her body. It wasn't exactly a dress or robe, because it moved and fluttered around her in a feminine fashion, but could shape to her body when she needed to move quickly or exert herself. The clothing was just as exquisite as the rest of the planet, but she preferred being naked, at least for the moment.

"Are you preparing to nap?"

She shook her head, though she often napped in the afternoon. Right then, she was energized rather than enervated. "I wouldn't mind lying down on the bed though, especially if I had company."

He moved quickly to shed his flowing gold garment, having eschewed the khaki body armor from the time they had arrived at the palace. In seconds, they were naked together, and he strode toward her.

Jory stood still as Zandar dropped to his knees, holding her breath as she expected his mouth to go between her legs. Instead, Zandar rested his cheek against her slightly swelling abdomen before turning his head to press a kiss below her belly button, perhaps an inch or two above where their child was growing.

It was a tender, touching gesture, and as she ran her hands through his long silver hair, Jory couldn't help the words that sprang to her lips. "I love you, Zandar."

He stilled for a long second, though his arms wrapped even tighter around her as he pulled her nearer. Then he looked up at her, his purple eyes shining. "I love you as well, Princess Jory. I knew I wanted you from the moment I saw you, even when I still thought you were Chiondri. I perhaps briefly entertained the idea of running away with you and keeping you from my brother, and then we crashed."

Her heart sang with joy in his declaration, and she knelt slightly to wrap her arms around his shoulders the best she could, cupping the back of his head with one hand as she played with his hair. "You mean were scheming to keep me even before you believed I was Jory and not Chiondri?"

He chuckled. "Scheming is too harsh a word, Princess Jory. I simply entertained the notion of not returning you. When you told me you weren't her, I wanted to believe it very badly. I allowed myself to be persuaded, and I am thrilled I listened to you."

"It's always a nice change when you listen to me," she said with gentle snarkiness. A second later, Jory squealed as he surged to his feet, lifting her into his arms and striding to the bed. He dropped her a little less than gently on the soft mattress that adhered to her body like a cloud.

Zandar dropped down atop her, bracing his weight on his arms, and his mouth ravished hers. Their lovemaking was frantic and fast-paced the first time around, neither of them able to get enough of the other. After their first orgasms, they slowed down and made love at a more leisurely pace.

Afterward, he held her against him with his hand on her stomach, his thumb rubbing lightly under her bellybutton. Jory was almost asleep when his whispered words penetrated the blissful haze from sexual satiety.

"Bond with me, Jory. Stay and be my princess, and then my queen some day. Bear me children and make my life much happier than it would be without you."

All traces of sleep fled, and she rolled over to face him. Logic warred with what her heart wanted, and she decided logic could be damned. It didn't matter if she'd only known him two weeks, or that he had uprooted her from everything she had ever known. Her love had been galaxies away, and if he hadn't sought her out—even though he'd actually been looking for Chiara in the beginning—they never would have met. "I would be pleased to bond with you, Zandar."

THE BONDING CEREMONY was similar to an earth wedding in some ways, including a gathering of friends and family. Jory had burst into tears when Prince Kendrick personally delivered her mother from Earth two days before the wedding, having taken a break from his pursuit of Chiondri to fulfill the mission and witness his brother's forthcoming bonding.

She had closeted herself with the other woman in the suite assigned to her mother, explaining the entire situation for hours on end. Her mother had initially been confused at being abducted from Earth, but after learning Jory was there and expecting her grandchild, and planning to stay on Karadis with a handsome alien prince, Bethany had quickly adapted and decided she would stay as well. It was a great comfort to have her mother sitting on the front row of the chairs arranged for the guests.

There were differences to the bonding ceremony, of course, and one of those was she stood at the front of the gathering as she waited for Zandar to come to her. The sight of him in all his naked glory made her heart race and her panties damp. Jory stifled a giggle.

Not that she was wearing any panties. The bonding ceremony consisted of exactly two garments. Each participant wore a sash around their waist that would be tied to the other's by the celebrant joining them after they had declared their intent to bond for life.

It had been daunting to stand in front of strangers in all her curvy glory, wearing only a golden scrap of material around her waist, but most of the guests also wore very little. She wasn't certain of the origin of the tradition, or why the guests were practically naked too, but it was better to be among a bunch of naked people than to be the only one.

Zandar strode through the crowd, because there wasn't actually an aisle like they would have for a traditional Earth wedding. He stopped to exchange greetings with guests, who wished him well and offered up gifts for the prosperity of their union. Per custom, he left the guests with his brother, who was the equivalent of his best man, before turning to her.

When he reached her, he dropped to his knees, and she did the same, having been coached by her cultural tutor. They joined hands, and she made her vows to be faithful and belong to him, and he repeated the same, including his promise to be only hers.

When they had finished, the celebrant took their sashes, tied the ends together, and they were joined in a bonding that was more permanent than an Earth marriage. Very few Karadisians ever broke their bond, and none entered into the union lightly. Jory knew it was almost unheard of to bond with someone she had only known two weeks—well, four weeks now, since it had taken a while to plan the bonding ceremony—but she was completely confident in the match.

As she got to her feet with his assistance, due to her large stomach, she leaned against her husband...bond–mate, she mentally corrected, and put her hand on her belly where their son was kicking. The healer had determined the gender last week, along with providing an estimate of her being roughly eighteen weeks pregnant by Earth standards.

It was difficult to guess when their little one would arrive, though it would be only a matter of weeks. She was looking forward to the birth, though not the pain, and giving Zandar the first of many children.

Most of all, she was looking forward to living happily ever after with her magenta-skinned alien bond-mate as his Princess Jory.

Epilogue

FREYDON LEANED BACK in his chair and smiled in satisfaction. He hadn't had a blatant hand in that match, but from the minute the real princess had fled, he'd helped guide Chiondri to Earth as a place to hide. He'd ensured she could obtain different credentials and have a chance to flee an arranged marriage. He knew there would be a happy ending for Chiondri in her future, but she had firstly been a means to bring Jory and Zandar together.

He turned to his files, knowing his work with the Karadisians wasn't done yet. Zyan was next, and he was in for quite an adventure with his future mate. Quite an adventure indeed...

About Aurelia

Aurelia Skye is the pen name bestselling author Kit Tunstall uses when writing science fiction romance. It's simply a way to separate the myriad types of stories she writes so readers know what to expect with each "author."

If you enjoyed this story and would like to receive notifications of new releases or access bonus chapters for your favorite books, please join my Mailing List[1]**. You'll also receive free books just for joining. If you prefer to receive notifications for just one, or a few, of Kit's pen names, you'll have the option to select which lists to subscribe to at signup.**

---

1. http://kittunstall.com/newsletter/

Did you love *Princess By Mistake*? Then you should read *Hooked*[2] by
Aurelia Skye!

If you think you know the story of "Peter Pan," think again. Wendy
Darling is a disgruntled employee at Lost Boys Clubhouse on planet
Neverland and technically involved with Peter Pan, but he's too busy
for her and always flirting with Tink. He's also totally immature and
refuses to grow up, so that's why she's leaving him. The arrival of James
Hook, in search of something Pan stole from him, derails her plans to
return to New London when he kidnaps her and takes her aboard the
Jolly Roger. As they set off on an adventure that spans the galaxy while
evading Admiral Croc, who's on James's tail, Wendy soon realizes she
doesn't need a boy when she can have a man.

---

2. https://books2read.com/u/bxZpPJ

3. https://books2read.com/u/bxZpPJ

Also by Aurelia Skye

Alien Baby Pact
Baby For The Brundle Commander
Baby For The Grimlock General
Baby For The Palantir Chief
Baby For The Alphan Captain

Celestial Mates
Wrong Place, Right Mate
Destined For The Drakari Warlords

Cybernetic Hearts
Mated To The Cyborg General
Claimed By The Cyborg Commander
Fated For The Cyborg Officer
Meant For The Cyborg Captain
Baby For The Cyborg General
Cybernetic Hearts: Complete Series

Dazon Agenda
Written In The Stars
Alien's Babies
Diplomatic Affairs
Moon Madness
Across The Stars
Emperor's Assassin Bride
Dazon Agenda: Complete Collection

Future Fairytales
Hooked

Harrow Bay
Hell Gates & Hot Flashes
Nightmares & Night Sweats
Warlocks & Wrinkles
Love Spells & Liver Spots
Phantasms & Presbyopia
Vampires & Varicose Veins
Mermaids & Mood Swings
Séances & Sagging Skin
Necromancy & Knee Pains
Marids & Memory Loss
Devil Deals & Dizzy Spells
Happy Endings & New Beginnings
Harrow Bay, Volume 1
Hellhounds & Mistletoe
Harrow Bay, Volume 2

Harrow Bay, Volume 3

Hell Virus
Catching Hell
Surviving Hell
Bleeding Hell
Raising Hell
Sharing Hell

Howls Romance
The Jaguar Alpha's Forbidden Lover

Northstar Shifters
Northstar Heir's Scarred Mate

Olympus Station
Station Commander's Surrogate
Alien Prince's Secret Baby
Security Agent's Alien Bartender
Olympus Station Compilation

SpicyShorts
Music In My Heart
Kilted Tentacle Monster: A Search for True Love

Sweet Escapes
Hook & Wendy

Three Crones Inn
Vastly Inn-proved
Ghastly Intentions
Ghostly Inn-heritance
Three Crones Inn Compilation

True North
True North #1: Death & Deception
True North #2: Rescued & Revelations
True North #3: Fire & Ice
True North #4: Enemies & Lovers
True North #5: Truth & Tiranog
True North #6: Fight & Flight
True North #7: Love & Loss

Wounded Warriors
Relentless
Marked
Justice
Wounded Warriors Collection
Hunted

Standalone

Reluctant Companion
Princess By Mistake
Fire Lord's Assistant
True North
Dragon Laird's Witch
Alien General's Rebel Consort
Tempted By Demons
Enemy Combatant
Grotesquerie
Mistaken Bounty